Shimmerfish

BETHANY BROWNING

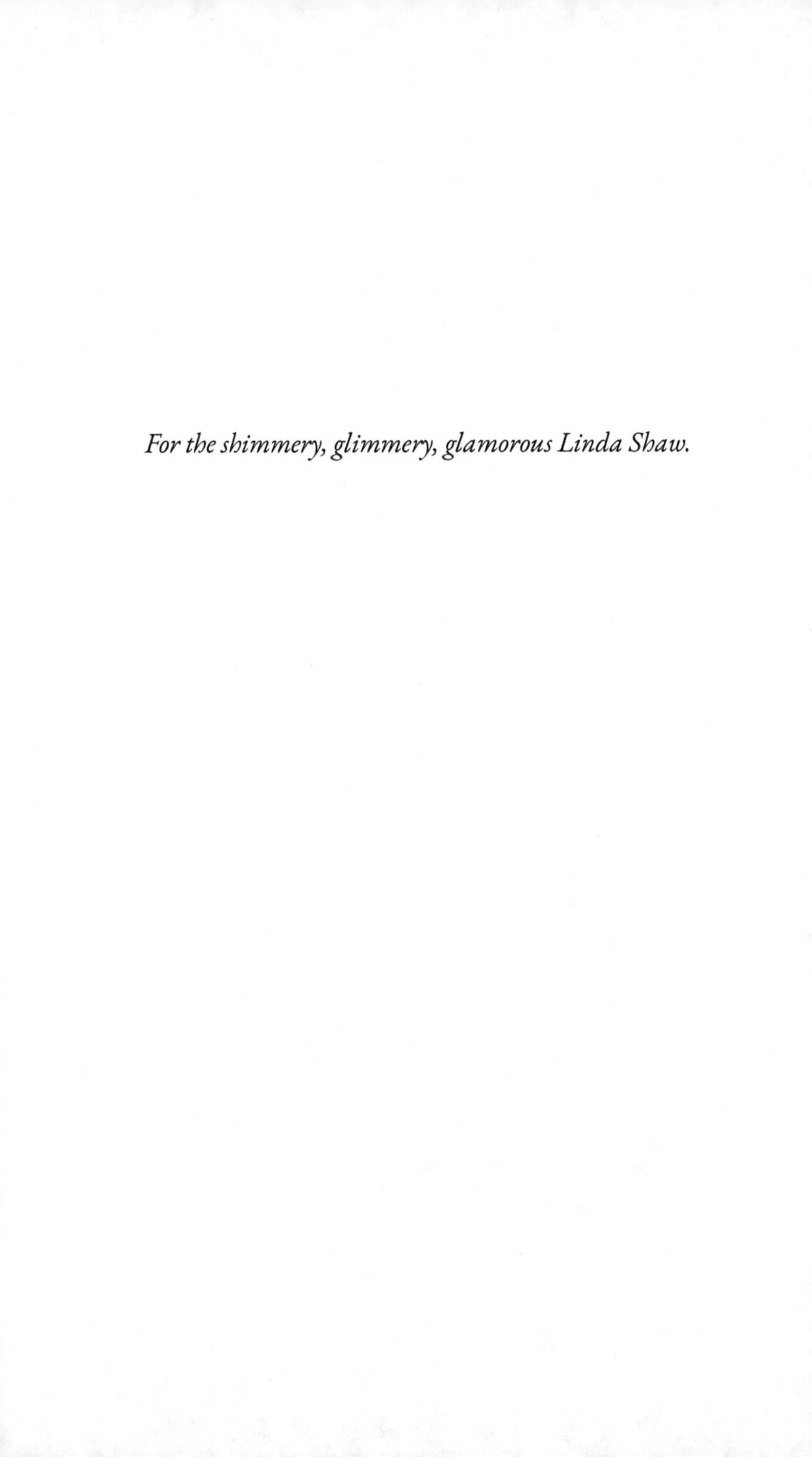

For the shimmery, glimmery, glamorous Linda Shaw.

You Should Know

I'd been dead before.

Woke up and walked home three miles.

I was warm—*I was warmth*—and there was a gentle tug in my middle section, as if someone was bringing me along with nothing more than a string of spider silk.

After my eyes flickered open, all I saw was Momma leaning over me, looking like she'd sucked on a lemon.

Her head was backlit by the high-noon sun, a blazing halo. I squinted against the shine. I put my hands over my ears to dull the booming sounds of the universe groaning and shifting under its own weight.

I could taste colors.

Not as fun as you might think.

"You done?" she said. "Let's go."

I'd been hit by a kid on a moped. Jumped the curb and spun me into the ground, clocking my head on a light post on the way down.

Momma didn't care. People like us were always getting knocked around.

"Keep your head down," she said, yanking me up by my wrist and dragging me along the dirt road away from Winn-Dixie. "Security's onto us."

There was a purloined pound of bacon in the waistband of my jeggings.

But there was no security. Momma'd made it up to keep me hustling. We lifted stuff all the time and had never been caught. Hell, that ratchet store barely had lightbulbs, much less their own action team.

My head throbbed and my mind fogged over. I was half in another dimension. I put one foot in front of the other until I was fully earthbound again.

Other than nodding when Momma told me to go wash the blood off, I never said nothing about it to no one.

The other time I thought I might be dead, Momma wasn't near when I came to. She'd been in the dirt for months. The real death you don't come back from. I was alone, in the woods, goose egg on the crown of my head, blood on my lips, scrapes on my knuckles, nothing to eat or drink, and no home to go back to.

I was missing my right middle fingernail.

Couldn't stop staring at it. My finger looked so...vulnerable.

Never realized how loud the sound of my own inhale and exhale was, not until I had to hide it. Not until Rutter chased me into the woods, did what he did, and left me for dead.

But I wasn't dead this time, was I? Knocked into next week, maybe. But not dead.

I knew the difference.

I cocooned myself in an entanglement of kudzu and listened to the catalytic whirr of the cicadas and the roar of the trucks on the same two-lane highway I'd eventually take out of town.

Rutter's smell lived in my nostrils. Pemmican made with game meat. Stale Coors. A whiff of Winstons.

I waited there, long past the time any medical professional

would recommend, to make certain Rutter thought I was good and dead.

When the time was right, I emerged.

Chapter One

"I remind myself of two things every day. One, all humans have troubles, pain, and fear. And two, slipping into a non-human form doesn't prevent suffering, but it sure can help you heal."—Shimmerfish

If Dr. Birdsong had warned me I'd be climbing onto the roof of a cinder block building at the ass-end of BobbiLu Beauregard Highway twice a week, I might've sought employment at the Holy Roller Rink-a-Rama instead.

"*Baby killer.*"

"*Filthy dyke.*"

"*Dick-eating slut.*"

They shouted those words at me every day, though I never sussed out how a body could be both a filthy dyke and a dick-eating slut. Guess I should've finished high school.

"I wouldn't even be up here if y'all didn't think it was funny to snap the second 'W' off our *Women's Whole Health* sign," I'd holler down to the scrum.

"Jezebel! Harlot! Uterus-haver!"

That one? With the ten-dollar vocabulary? Meet my boss, Dr. Robin Birdsong.

"Alright, enough," I said, once I'd touched my second-hand Skechers back onto terra firma. "I know you think it's funny, Dr. Birdsong, but these people have potato salad for brains. All mayo. No seasoning."

"You like this?" Dr. Birdsong said, wiggling a poster board sign. It read: *Don't like abortion? Don't get one.*

"I've seen better," I said.

"How dare you?" she asked with a wink.

"Besides, you need to get inside on account of we have patients scheduled."

Dr. Birdsong dropped her sign to the ground, turned to face the protesters, raised her two middle fingers high into the air and said, "For the thousandth time, we don't do abortions here, you lunatics!"

Then, conspiratorially, "But if any of you ladies need medical care or have any questions about what your uncle did to you, Women's Whole Health can help you sort it out."

Someone spit on Dr. Birdsong and she wiped it off her chin, one hand still holding up the middle finger.

I'd learned on week one not to engage the frothy-mouthed fetus fanatics. Explaining Women's Whole Health offered pap smears, birth control, STI prevention, pre-natal, postpartum, and well-baby care was like wrestling a pig. You both get filthy, and the pig likes it.

The people who had nothing better to do than harass a doctor who provided the most basic women's services neither understood nor cared about the distinction. The only thing these zealots understood was any female who allowed a doctor to eyeball her Merry Christmas without buying her dinner first is a slatternly hoe-bag.

"Do as I say, not as I do, Amy Jay," Doctor Birdsong said to me as she was putting on her white coat. "It's not professional of me to behave in this manner."

"I know," I said. "You're the least professional person I've met in my life and my dead momma once let a live squirrel loose in her boss's Durango."

True story.

I'd met Dr. Birdsong on my first day in town, right after I'd stolen my dead momma's measly state life insurance payout and fled to where I thought my latest derelict stepdaddy Rutter wouldn't find me. I pulled my momma's vee-dub-ya right off the highway, limped into Women's Hole Health, and got the medical care I knew I needed. And so much more.

Dr. Birdsong was so nice to me I never wanted to leave. Looked me in the eye. Pulled a tick out of my scalp and rubbed cream on my chigger bites. Believed everything I told her, even the obvious lies. Offered me a tissue when it looked like I might squirt a tear. Wrapped a glow-in-the dark bandage emblazoned with stars and comets around my missing fingernail. Handed me a juice box.

"I know, I know. You're an adult, and this is a child's bandage," she said, still holding my hand in hers. "But sometimes, when we're injured especially, it's fine to have some silliness. How's your Hawaiian Punch treating you?"

"It's real good," I said, slurping up the final bit and realizing how hungry I was.

"When was the last time you saw a physician?" she asked.

I thought about it. I'd seen the school nurse a few times for splinters and skinned knees.

"My dead momma took me to urgent care once when I swallowed an ice cube whole."

Dr. Birdsong laughed. I didn't.

"Oh. You're serious," she said. "Oh, yes. Okay. Explains some stuff. When was your last period?"

I shrugged.

"I'm going to draw blood and send it to a lab. Do you remember if you've ever had blood drawn?"

"I don't remember," I said. My shoulders tightened.

"Unclench," she said. "No need to worry. It's not unusual for young women your age to be seeing a doctor like me for the first time. It's not your fault. And everything's going to be peachy."

She fiddled around with things, snapped a pair of new gloves on, and kept me laughing the whole time so I didn't even notice she'd slipped the needle in.

"All done," she said. "You look healthy. Strong teeth. Rosy cheeks. But it's good to check. Those results will be available in a few days."

Dr. Birdsong's kindness was like easing into a warm tub of soapy water after a long trek from town on a cold day. After I'd died with a bag of bacon in my drawers.

"Want me to fix your sign?" I asked when Dr. Birdsong told me to get dressed. "I don't have much money, but I can fix your sign if you want."

"Would you?" she asked. Her eyes lit up like I'd told her Santa Claus had left her everything in his will.

And then, "The bump on your head though. And your limp. I couldn't ask it. Might be unethical. Or dangerous. Or both. Both. Yeah. Probably both."

"I don't mind," I said. "How long's your sign been vandalized?"

"Since my receptionist went to her ease. She was ninety years old and held together with rusty nails and vinegar. I can't climb up there because of my vertigo, but she'd shimmy up a ladder fast as a treed bear."

She was barely done speaking before I'd exited the building, wrestled the squeaky old ladder to the side of the building, and clambered up. I didn't want her telling me no. I wanted to help, and I did.

When I dropped down from the roof the first time, pain shot

from my leg into the top of my head. Dr. Birdsong might've been right about taking it easy.

As I walked—or staggered—it off, Dr. Birdsong offered me a job. Right after she handed me a bright blue gel cap for what she called inflammation.

My bruises healed and so did the rest of me. Blood work checked out. No pregnancy. No STI.

And Dr. Birdsong kept me snug under her wing.

Chapter Two

HOW TO INTRODUCE YOURSELF ON LAND
    •Smile.
    *•Waggle your tail (even if it's a hot, soupy, sweaty mess—*remember* this is your dream.)*
    •Say, "My name is Shimmerfish. What's yours?"
    •Mnemonic devices help you remember names!!
    •Tell children they are "fin-tastic," "mer-mazing," and "spe-shell."
    •Answer all questions with cheer in your voice.
    •Blow kisses to your new friends as they leave. 💋

—Shimmerfish

"Only five bomb threats on the voicemail this morning," I said on a soggy summer Monday. "But there was one guy who knew your home address."

The doctor made an impressed face.

"Only five?" she asked.

"Everyone was at the God, Guns, and Glory Jamboree this weekend," I said. "Too busy stocking up on slaughter machines to fuss over imaginary piles of rotting embryos."

"You know what I like about you, Amy Jay," Dr. Birdsong said. "You put things together. You've got a gift."

Dr. Birdsong was warm and weird. She had a habit of acting like she'd been someone's best friend their whole life, even when they just met. I thought she was funny, but her patients didn't know what to make of her.

One time she told a pregnant lady, "When you come back for your checkup, I'll show you how we train the storks. Bring stale bread."

Because of Dr. Birdsong, I didn't hate my life. I didn't love it, neither, but I was working through some stuff. I existed in a divot between happiness and misery where there was no feeling whatsoever. Every day happened like the one before it. Things were likely to stay that way until I stepped into traffic or was eaten from the inside out by a ravenous tumor.

Or Rutter would find me and finish me off.

I was afraid of most things. Always looking over my shoulder, for good reason.

I think it's called irony, but I was safer there at that clinic with the howling protesters in the parking lot, in this tiny, backward town, than I'd ever been before. Ain't no woman-hating zealot outside this building worse than any normal day in back in my heritage family home.

Terror's a spectrum, I'd learned.

So, when those teary-eyed women came through our doors after running a gauntlet of abuse to get their yearlies, I knew how to steady them. I knew how it felt to have no one to turn to, to be in trouble you can't speak about. I could feel their need to be seen in my bones. It was a gnawing thing, made possible only when you've tried to express yourself, only to be dismissed, ignored, and criminalized.

I knew them. They didn't know I knew them or how I knew them, and they never asked. But I did. I got it.

Working there was the first thing I'd done worth taking pride in.

By lunch time, Dr. Birdsong was outside pelting the protesters with handfuls of rubbers.

"You want to prevent abortion? Cover your ding-dongs!"

"Is that the medical term?" I asked, and we had a good giggle over it.

I'd go scoop the leftover condoms out of the parking lot later, a perverted Easter egg hunt. Put them in a bowl at the reception desk like they were candy. Offered them up to everyone who came and left.

This was normal.

It was also normal for Dr. Birdsong to enter the building with her arm wrapped around the shoulder of a crying girl close to my age.

What wasn't normal was when Dr. Birdsong swished past front desk without so much as a how-dee-doo. She shepherded a young woman into her office and closed the door.

Time passed, and the patients in the waiting room were getting restless. Some had to return to work; some school.

Others had to get home before their husbands did so they could rinse. Nothing like a splat of speculum goo in the underpants to convince a redneck who's never heard of a pap smear his woman's two-timing him.

They ended up at a different doctor then.

I knocked on the doctor's door.

"Come in," Dr. Birdsong called.

The crying girl turned to face me.

"Amy Jay, this is my niece, Phoebe. My sister Dove's girl."

Phoebe was a beautiful crier. Her face was pale, like a stone statue in a history book, and her aqua eyes shimmered with tears. One side of her head was shaved, and the line was accentuated by a delicate flower-vine tattoo, kinda like the trumpet vine that snaked along my dead momma's back fence. Her hair, on the side she let it grow out, tumbled down her right shoulder in big, bouncy, waves.

She had a small turquoise nose piercing. She smelled like pipe tobacco and lilacs.

Might as well have shot me in the sternum with an elephant cannon.

My knees turned to speculum goo; my tongue felt hot and swollen in my mouth.

Dr. Birdsong looked watery-eyed. "I haven't seen this young woman since...well over a decade now, I'm sorry to say. She looks quite different. But she's still a piece of my heart."

Phoebe beamed at Dr. Birdsong's adoring gaze.

I understood.

"Phoebe's going to be staying in town for a bit," the doctor continued. "Family stuff. She'd like to stay busy until it's time for her to go. You okay with giving her some jobs to do around here?"

"Sure," I said.

My neck tingled.

"Thanks," Phoebe said, with a slight southern accent, her voice softer than I imagined it would be.

"What a nice little family we have here at Women's Whole Health," Dr. Birdsong said. "I have to get back to work. Those paps aren't going to smear themselves, right, ladies?"

Chapter Three

"Safety first. Never go in the water alone. Never perform at an event alone. Always have your pirate with you. Take breaks when you need them. You can't be a mermaid if you're dead." —Shimmerfish

I'd been jobbed up by Dr. Birdsong for about a week or a little more before she realized something was off.

Everything I was doing should've set alarms off all over, and that it didn't set alarms off all over should've set off an alarm for ME.

But I had no idea what I was doing.

"Amy Jay, is everything okay at home?" she asked one evening as we were closing up.

I shot her a look like, *"You know everything's not okay at home, which is why I fell in here last week out of the clear blue sky."*

"You can talk to me about anything," she said. "I know you're a private person. But if you need help, you should let me know."

My life had been nothing but one long secret. My dead

momma constantly told me to pipe down, stay quiet, don't discuss nothing with nobody. No one is your friend and everyone's out to get you. I wasn't about to unravel my training in one fell swoop. Even if Dr. Birdsong was already the person I trusted more than anyone else in the world.

I stared at her, my mouth a thin line.

"I'll let you get back to whatever you were doing," she said. She tapped some folders on the reception desk and disappeared into her office.

After I'd locked up, I motored my dead momma's vee-dub-yah to the Fill n' Rest truck stop out at the end of where BobbiLu Beauregard Highway veers off to become Route 2. I'd been spending my nights there on account of I could get a burger and a shower before I slept in the backseat.

"This is not safe, Amy Jay," was the first thing Dr. Birdsong said to me when I walked out into the parking lot, hair still wet from a two-dollar shower.

"What are you doing here?" was how I responded.

"I suspected you were living in your car, dear," she said to me. "I don't want to pry into your personal situation. But I think you should come with me. Come on now. Get in your bug and follow me back into town."

I did as I was told, and within fifteen minutes, I was standing next to Dr. Birdsong on a sidewalk in front of a nondescript gray building one block off Main Street.

"I saw this FOR RENT sign earlier today," Dr. Birdsong said. "And I realized I'd never offered you this part of your compensation package."

"What are you talking about?" I asked.

"I called the number, and the landlady is on her way."

Sure enough, a woman appeared. She unlocked the door.

"What do you think?" Dr. Birdsong asked. She was trying to put a happy face on it but suffice it to say, the only person who would think this was an acceptable place to live would be someone like me, who'd been hiding out in her dead momma's car for two weeks after having spent god-knows-how-long living underneath a shrub in the woods.

"I like it," I lied.

Dr. Birdsong handed over first and last month's rent. I was to be quiet, not smoke, not have pets or parties, and if I ever broke any of those rules, the landlord said she'd padlock the door and keep all my stuff.

I had no stuff, so this seemed fine for me.

Dr. Birdsong continued to speak as she signed some paperwork on a clipboard. "What I mean when I say this is part of your compensation, is the clinic has a fund for employees to help with things like rent."

She was lying, and I loved her for it.

"You need essentials," she said. "Don't be afraid to speak up."

"Thank you," I said. I couldn't think of anything else to say.

"I'll call you tonight to check in. I don't think I have your number." She pulled out her phone and asked me for my digits.

"No phone," I said.

"Oh. Fine," Dr. Birdsong said, flustered. She slipped her phone back into her bag. "Your position comes with a cell phone. I'll get it for you tomorrow."

"A phone is part of my compensation?"

"It is," she said with an overdramatic nod. "You need help bringing anything in?"

"No ma'am," I said. "Shouldn't take but a few minutes."

Dr. Birdsong seemed hesitant to leave, like she wasn't sure this was going to work out. But she couldn't stay all night. With much conflict in her eyes, she left.

My new pad was one room with a shower and a toilet behind a curtain in the northwest corner, a kitchen with a small fridge, a sink, and a microwave. The floor was concrete; the ceiling popcorn. It had been an employee break room or something similar at one point.

It was home, whether I wanted it to be or not.

First thing I did was close the curtains. Never knew who might be looking in.

Chapter Four

"The harder you work, the more it looks like magic. Never let them see the struggle." —Shimmerfish

Phoebe was seated at the front desk when I arrived the following morning, looking for all the world like an alternate-universe mouse-house princess. She wore sea-green leggings covered with what looked like fish scales and a silver sequined tank top. Hair fluffed enough to make you wonder if she woke up like that or if she styled it to give the impression she woke up like that. Her hands and arms sparkled with costume jewelry. Pearls. Beads. Crystals.

"How do you deal with those wingnuts every single day?" she asked as I let the back door close behind me.

This was rocky terrain. I wasn't accustomed to talking about myself. I never answered questions about the clinic.

I had to take a beat to decide whether I'd tell Phoebe the truth about how I maintained a shred of sanity amidst a daily onslaught of verbal abuse.

The insults were water off a duck's back. My dead momma and foul-mouthed stephusbands turned me deaf to threats.

"Back door," I said.

"Nice," Phoebe said, her eyes twinkling in a way that suggested my statement had a double meaning.

I blushed.

"It's not easy," I said, taking off her backpack and shoving it under the check-in counter. "But it's better to see what your enemies are doing."

"When they go dark, we worry," Phoebe said.

My stomach dropped a little. I'd been thinking the same thing about my own situation, but the way Phoebe worded it made it make more sense. I hadn't heard nothing from my enemy since I disappeared. And I didn't feel any better about any of it. In fact, not knowing was scarier than knowing.

"Good turn of phrase," I said to her. "It's true. As long's I can see them, I can respond to them. Protect myself."

"Right? Like it would be terrifying if you came in one morning and they weren't there. You'd be all, *what are they up to?* Still, all this threatening negative energy calls for a spell."

I took my seat behind the reception desk. It would be tight back there all day with the two of us. I didn't mind. She smelled so good.

"I'm sorry if you're confused," I said. "But this is a place of medicine. Not magic."

"You're funny," she said. I was relieved she knew I was joking —not a lot of people got my deadpan delivery. Caused problems for me. But Phoebe caught on right away.

"My spells are serious, though," she said. "We're going to protect this place, and you can help."

"You're a witch?" I asked.

"And a mermaid. I'm a mermaid witch. A mer-witch. Different from a sandwich. A little humor."

She tossed the word 'mer-witch' like anyone else would say

they'd had pink eye once or could do a cartwheel. Natural as anything.

"I've never met a witch or mermaid—or a mer-witch —before."

"Come over after work and I'll show you," Phoebe said. "Help me do the spell."

My dead momma and her parade of partners weren't much for church-going, unless it was to drunkenly crash their exes' weddings. But I remembered something about witchcraft being a mortal sin and mermaids being fish and, therefore, disgusting.

Not a chance in hell I was saying no to this.

"Sounds awesome," I said, forgetting I was in hiding.

"Fin-tastic," she said. "You can call me Anemone. My mer-name."

Chapter Five

"Your mer-name is meant to last forever. Try a few before settling. Find the mer-name that fits you like a custom-made tail."—Shimmerfish

My dead momma's maiden name was Vicky White. She married my daddy and became Vicky White Black. I never knew him. Then there was a whole bunch of others who came and went, and each one was worse than the one before. The last one she married, the one I was still running from, was named Pink. Rutter Pink. He's the one who took her to Myrtle Beach, where a resort umbrella achieved lift off north of the SkyWheel, skittered forty yards down the beach and found purchase in her navel. It burst out her back after severing her lumbar spine.

As my dead momma bled out on the sand, the pointy end of an umbrella pole plunged into some vital organs and jammed out her sacrum, her name was Vicky White Black Pink.

Her violent death left me and a man I hardly knew living in the same house.

He said he owned my dead momma's house now.

Said he owned me.

No more school.

Fine by me.

I cooked hamburger, scrubbed pots, set the roach traps, emptied ashtrays, fed the strays.

Never enough.

He wanted what my dead momma gave him, too.

I ran.

He chased.

I hunkered down in the woods surrounding my dead momma's house. Watched until Rutter drove off somewhere. Snuck in, cleaned myself up. Took some things.

"Bye, Momma," I said as I grabbed the keys to her vee-dub-ya off the counter. And it might have been the head injury, but I'll be good goddamned if I didn't hear my momma's raspy growl tell me to pull the top drawer on her dresser.

Rutter had cashed momma's paltry life insurance at the Check-4-Cash and left a wad of bills the exact right size for my grubby fingers in her top drawer.

I took every dollar without so much as a thought to how Rutter might respond.

I thanked my dead momma for the heads up. Stole her vee-dub-ya and zoomed off to find the best hiding spot I could.

But I've been fearing his shadow ever since. And I had no plans to mention it to nobody.

* * *

I was glad it was a busy day because I was too nervous to speak to Anemone outside of reminding her what to say when she answered the phone and telling her how to spell certain names.

Anemone whisked out with *sea you soon* and an exaggerated wink to make sure I got the pun.

Dr. Birdsong was in her battle station out front, calling one of the regular protesters a weeping wart hole, while I escaped through the back door to avoid the whole thing.

Normal. Day.

Only this time, I was headed to Dr. Birdsong's house after work.

Would we all hang out together? Order pizza? Give each other facials?

Did Dr. Birdsong know about mer-witching?

I hadn't thought this through. I could barely make eye contact with anyone, much less spend an entire evening trying to be normal. Or mer-mal or whatever.

Too awkward. Shouldn't be hanging out at the boss lady's house. Last time my dead momma went to a boss's house, she set a dead cat on fire on his doorstep while I sat in her old vee-dub-ya and watched. No good comes from going to the boss's house.

Besides, once Anemone got to know me, she wouldn't like me.

Someone like Anemone—gorgeous, unique, passing through —would bore of me soon enough.

I was none of those things. Opposite, in fact. Didn't even know how to pretend. I've always looked older than my age. Something about the dark, weary circles under my eyes and my post-puberty body gave folks the impression I was more mature than I was. Maturity didn't make me pretty or interesting, but it did give me problems. With both men and women, if I'm honest.

My armpits were damp. My hands clammy. My joints felt off; my neck popped. Nothing sat right, and I needed to get out.

I reminded myself to breathe, then flipped a U-ey in the street to head home. Nothing there but four walls and some ninety-nine cent ramen.

I heard my dead momma's voice reassuring me: "People you work with ain't your friends."

Hard agree, I thought. I needed to keep myself out of the spotlight, and tagging along with a living doll who called herself a mer-witch wasn't the best way to go about it.

Then, a bus. In my rearview.

A regular-type school bus with the big windows, stop sign, and everything. But turquoise.

The headlights blinked, illuminating the interior of my dead momma's vee-dub-ya like lightning flashes.

Rutter, was all I could think.

I had to be quick.

And smart.

I gripped the steering wheel and gritted my teeth. Only a few more turns and I thought I'd be able to give this bus and whoever was driving it the slip.

The bus honked, a deafening sound like a freight train caused my stomach to twist.

The vibrations cut through me.

Protesters, maybe?

They'd found me. Had they bird-dogged me when I pulled out of the parking lot at the clinic? Were they hoping to find where I lived?

Was the bus filled with assassins from the Bible Believers' Church of the Well-Armed Christ, standing by to pop a slug in my forehead?

"Don't panic," I said out loud, the words getting stuck on my dry tongue.

More honking. More lights.

I waved and rounded my shoulders to show I was harmless. "*Haiii,*" I whispered.

The driver was flailing around, trying to get my attention.

Maybe if I pulled over, the bus would go around?

I steered the car off the road and settled on the shoulder.

The bus pulled up alongside me.

I braced for an attack.

"Get in, Loser," Anemone called out from the driver's seat. "We're going to the lake."

Chapter Six

"Stop comparing yourself to other mermaids! Some have more money than you, others have better moves, are prettier, can hold their breath longer. But you are the only you. And you are all you've got. Love yourself."—Shimmerfish

My dead momma didn't waste time between men. She believed it was her moral obligation to provide a loving home for strays.

"All men are feral," she said. "It's my job to domesticate them."

We were between stephusbands when she said it.

"Couldn't you volunteer at the shelter instead?" I asked.

She laughed so hard I thought she might puncture a lung.

I beamed.

Making my dead momma laugh was my best good feeling. It didn't happen often. Looking back, seems like she only laughed when we were alone together.

Except one time.

Before Rutter, there was Gib Dickey.

He'd left his wife for Momma, which she thought made her

special. Made most of his money stealing tools and supplies from construction sites and then re-selling them.

"Why don't you have a real job?" I asked him once. Momma's eyes got wide. She shook her head back and forth. A warning.

But Gib wasn't fazed. He told me he worked for a world-class asshole once. Made them all work overtime without extra pay.

"Then he wanted us to come to his kid's eighth birthday party and bring presents," Gib said. "I told him there was no way in hell I was going to a child's birthday party for work without pay."

"What did he do?"

"He got real close to my face and said he was going to fire me if I didn't go. I said fine. I'll go."

"You backed down?" I asked.

"In a manner of speaking," he said. "I went to the party. Brought a Bratz doll. Kid was thrilled. Boss man was happy. That night, I fucked the boss man's mom. I won."

Gib had airs, which my dead momma liked at first. He demanded he be treated like royalty. From what I learned, being treated like royalty meant Gib Dickey didn't pay for nothing.

He'd stolen and re-sold something called a Kubota and had some cash burnin' a hole in his Levi's. "Let's celebrate at Belly Busters. It's all-you-can-eat trotters night."

Imagine my surprise. Gib Dickey, who'd never released a dime from his closed fist, was taking us out.

I ran to his truck faster than you could say trotters are pig feet. I loved Belly Busters. The walls were covered with funny posters that said stuff like *Sorry, We're Open* and *Today's Soup is Beer*. They had a mechanical bull I always begged to ride, Skee-ball, and air hockey. On your birthday, you'd get a cookie shaped like a man's big beer belly, complete with a navel. If you got there before it got busy, you'd get a table by the window where you could watch the geese on the lake. They rented out wave runners there, too, but we never got one.

I gobbled down as many trotters as I could, desperate to finish so I could try to win the stuffed unicorn I'd had my eye on for years. When I was ready to ask to be excused, the mood had shifted in our booth.

My dead momma was saying she was sorry they'd ever met.

Gib said he was leaving for Daytona to work the stock cars and she'd better be careful because he might not come back.

Then, she called him Gib Dickless. He got up, threw his napkin down on the table, and huffed out.

I knew better than to ask about Skee-ball.

Momma sobbed.

She wouldn't stop. Wouldn't look at me. Tore her napkin into tiny bits.

Then, the bill came.

I didn't have to read it to know we couldn't pay it.

The bill sat there, taunting us.

Momma looked at it. Then she caught my eye. Started crying again.

I wanted to play Skee-ball, but the timing wasn't right. And I couldn't leave Momma here crying. She looked so small.

Time passed.

People were too drunk to stay on the bull.

It was getting late; I had school the following morning.

Not like I loved school, but it was better than being at home most of the time.

This was mine to fix now. I knew what to do.

My tongue found a loose tooth. It was a new one; just beginning to give.

I pinched it between my thumb and forefinger. Wiggled it the tiniest bit.

It gripped. This tooth wasn't ready, but life doesn't let us wait for biology.

I worried it back and forth, increasing the intensity with purpose.

It started to give. My gums ached, but I continued to pull.

Throbbing, pulsating pain overtook me. My gums were raw and tender.

I continued to twist and pull, each yank loosening the tooth more and sending sharp stabs into the right side of my skull.

My mouth tasted like nickels.

One quick tug down.

The tooth was in my hand.

"*Bobba*," I said, blood burbling out of my mouth and dribbling down my chin.

She caught on. She laughed.

She nodded.

I screamed holy hell. Took a whole breath and screamed again.

"My baby!" my dead momma yelled. "She broke her tooth!"

Servers rushed over. I continued wailing. I made sure to spit out as much blood as I could. Blood dropped onto my shirt, looking like the patterns the school psychologist once used to read my mind.

Chaos. Momma yelled about what kind of establishment would hurt a child and she's gonna sue and we would not be paying this check, you'd be lucky if we don't send you the medical bills, all while grabbing the check, shoving it in her pocket, and ferrying me and my blood-filled mouth to the door.

"I'll be calling my lawyer," Momma shouted. She stepped on my foot, hard. I cried out.

"What is it, baby?" She made a big show of kneeling down to see what the trouble was. "Let me see in there."

I opened my mouth as wide as I could. I saw one of the servers recoil. The manager kept apologizing over and over again.

Momma looked up at the gathering crowd, her eyes wild. She loved this kind of thing.

"Her mouth is ruined! Ruined!" She started to cry, and I followed suit.

"Ma'am, we are so very sorry," the manager said, again. "Obviously, your meal is comped. And here are coupons for a free dessert next time you come back to Belly Busters."

She took the coupons. "It's the least you can do," she said. "We can't afford a dentist."

"Do you have any coupons for Skee-ball?" I asked. Thought it was worth a shot.

Momma grabbed my hand and gave it the shut-up squeeze.

"You'll be lucky if you ever see us here again," she said with a final flourish. She shoved me through the door and into the parking lot.

Dickless had left us with no car, so we walked home, all the time Momma with her arm around me, talking about how proud she was, and could you believe the look on their faces?

We laughed so hard she had to stop walking at one point.

I handed her the tooth.

She tossed it into the lake.

"You're too old for the tooth fairy," she said.

I was fine with it. I'd take Momma's laughter over a quarter from the tooth fairy any day. Plus, we got dessert coupons.

We arrived home around two in the morning.

Gib was gone.

I crawled into bed with my Momma and stroked her hair.

"What you did today, baby, was brave," she said, drowsiness in every word.

"I love you, Momma," I said, my mouth raw.

"I know you do," she said.

Three weeks later, she turned up with Rutter. Wooed him with free dessert coupons.

Chapter Seven

"Nothing meant for you will pass you by. You'll be a mermaid if it's your destiny. And it IS your destiny."—Shimmerfish

"Where were you off to?" Anemone asked, as if it was the funniest thing she'd ever seen. "Can't say I've ever had to run someone off the road to get them to hang out with me."

I'd calmed down from the very real terror of being attacked by either bloodthirsty evangelicals or an unhinged redneck with a score to settle and I found myself in a different dimension. One where a mer-witch drove a tropical-colored school bus and I would do anything to impress her.

"I forgot something at home," I lied.

I left Momma's vee-dub-ya parked right where it was and climbed aboard.

There was no passenger seat; this was a real school bus. I was sitting in the one seat behind her. If I leaned forward, I'd be able to bite her earlobe, which was a bizarre thought for me to have, but there we were.

I was glad she couldn't see how I was devouring the sight of her.

"That's not true. But it's okay," she said. "Something spooked you."

My cheeks burned at her observation. I wasn't accustomed to anyone picking apart my behaviors, unless it was the adults telling me to stop doing something or to start doing something. What were friends? I didn't know.

I also didn't remember seeing any girls at my school who looked, dressed, or acted like her. Anemone was confident, self-possessed, with an easygoing way. She wasn't intimidated by me.

She was beautiful in the traditional sense. High cheekbones, turned-up nose, everything well-proportioned. If she'd not had the half-shaved head, the tattoos, and the mer-clothes, you could have seen her getting crowned on any pageant stage in the southeast.

I looked at my old, stretched out T-shirt, one my dead momma had brought home from a work thing. It read, *Teamwork makes the dream work*. I took a sniff of it. Fusty, at best. I hadn't done too much laundry since I'd gotten here. I didn't know how to other than rinse my stuff in the sink and try to smooth out wrinkles as it dried.

There was nothing to say about myself, and if there was, I still don't think I could've gotten the words out. I pivoted the conversation to something where I could ask her questions.

"How is this yours?" I asked while admiring the dining booth, the cabinets, drawers spilling over with baubles and beads and other trinkets. Florid pink curtains provided privacy and a touch of girliness. I'd never seen any house, much less a bus, fixed up with such an array of eye-catching things. Being in here made me feel like a used-up rag.

"This is my school bus," Anemone said. "And I fixed it up myself."

"*School*. I get it. You don't live in here, do you?" I ran my hands over the kitchen containers on the tiny counter next to a working sink. I turned the sink on and off and tried to act cool.

"Like I was going to make you sit in that doctor's living room all night. Gawd."

I winced at her tone when she said *that doctor's*. I thought she should have been more respectful, but then I remembered people often have troubled history with their family members, no matter how nice everyone seems to be.

"It's cute how you all have bird names," I said. I'd been thinking about that all day, how three women in one family could all have this one thread in common. How sweet it must feel to be a part of a generational tradition, one you could pass down to your own daughter.

"What are you talking about?"

"Robin. Dove. Phoebe. All birds," I said. Her reaction was so snippy I decided against pointing out I've got a bird name—sort of —as well.

"Phoebe is a girls' name," she said with such emphasis I knew never to bring it up again.

We'd pulled into a camping spot on the shore of Lake Longago. She put the emergency brake on and joined me in the back of the bus.

"After you're done here, you're moving on to greener pastures?"

"More like calmer seas," she said. "Look." She swept her arm out like a game show hostess showing off a prize. "I love having a home on the road. I can always be near water. And this lake is so sparkly. But I have somewhere to be. Soon."

The lake looked like any other lake. Similar to the Belly Busters lake, which was used to cool the nuke plant. Nice enough until you realize the water's so warm, the only things that thrive there are leeches and some type of carp that tastes like a bagged fart unless you smother it in soy sauce.

I never considered the natural features of the local area to be awe-inspiring. Most of it was flat. Some pine trees. Shrubby plants and biting bugs as loud as they were big. Nothing to get worked up about. After my days and nights in the woods pretending to be dead, I'd lost the desire to be swept away by Mother Nature's beauty. Out there, all I'd had was dried blood, blackberry brambles, pill bugs, and throbbing pain.

But this bus—I'd never imagined something like it was possible.

"Mer-witching isn't a hobby for me," Anemone said. "It's my whole life. I choose to live in a world of color, dimension, magic, nature, and enchantments. I deserve abundance. My destiny is grandeur, exhalation, and everything sublime in the universe. *So mote it be.*"

Anemone reminded me of my dead momma's neighbor up the way. He went to the county clinic to have his anal fissures cauterized and when he woke up, he was fluent in Esperanto. Anemone might as well have been speaking a made-up language.

Mote?

I hung on every word like a fishhook into a lip.

"'*So mote it be*' is like saying amen," she said when she saw the look of confusion on my face. "I'm manifesting."

"Slow down," I said. "I'm going to need you to start from the beginning because I have no clue what you're saying to me."

Anemone got up for a second, took some items out of a drawer, and placed them on the built-in table between us. "Incense," she said. "This one is copal. Good for purification."

"You mean mer-ification?" I asked.

"Look at you," she said, mock-impressed. "I'm stealing that one."

She continued. "Copal also repels mosquitos, which is an added benefit for mermaids who find themselves near standing water. Which is frequent."

Pipe smell, explained, I thought as I watched the smoke thread and curl in the air.

"Tell me all about mer-witching," I said. "I'm your student."

"When I was eight or nine years old," she began. "My parents sent me to Florida for a beach Bible camp. I wasn't much of a swimmer, and I'd never seen the ocean before. But all the other kids were strong swimmers, and I wanted so bad to join them in the waves.

"And there's something about the ocean, right? You see it and you want to run into it, swim away until you find an island. At least that's how it was for me."

"I've never been to the ocean," I said. I thought of my dead momma in Myrtle Beach. I wondered if she ever wanted to take me, or if I'd ever see it for myself.

"You must go. You must," she said. She put both hands on mine, scooting the copal aside as she reached across.

"Camp had a school bus like this one," she said. "Not all decorated, but you know what I mean. After a morning of discussing Jonah and the Whale, they drove us out to a wide, white-sand beach and released us. Everyone ran screaming toward the water, taking their shirts off and kicking their shoes into the sand as they went. I wasn't trying to stand out in any way, so I ran with them, right into the surf. I didn't know anything about waves. I thought the ocean was no more than a salty swimming pool. I got clobbered immediately. I didn't understand how the water would crash and then suck me out to sea."

I was on the edge of my seat. "What happened?"

"I don't even know. It's as if I wasn't even there."

I nodded. I'd learned how to let my mind float away so I wouldn't have to experience what was happening to my body. Became easy as flipping a switch after a while.

"I was overwhelmed," she continued. "Couldn't breathe. Exhausted. I could hear the others laughing and screaming. I knew they didn't know what was happening. I couldn't keep my head above water. I let go."

"Oh, no," I said. I hadn't realized I was chewing my thumb, and I stopped so she wouldn't think I was gross.

"I opened my eyes and looked around. The sun was blazing, and I could see the sand on the bottom of the ocean floor. Some gray fish found the bows on my swimsuit and nibbled them. They were cold as they bumped against me. I remember being thankful I'd been at Bible camp and found Jesus, so I'd go to heaven."

"Whoa."

"I know, right? But then, a swish. A flash of scales. A face. In front of mine."

"No way."

"Here's the thing." She motioned to her hair, her eyeliner, her tattoos. "This is all human lore."

"What do you mean?"

I didn't know this word, *lore*.

"The mermaid had a shimmering, colorful tail—like a rainbow trout—and long hair braided with shells and wrapped around bits of sea glass, coral, and animal bones. Our version ends there. Her upper body was covered in scales. Her eyes were yellow, and the pupils were vertical, like a goat's. Her nails," she waggled her acrylic blue nails at me. "Claws. Thick, black, and pointy as pins."

"Were you scared?"

"Shell, yeah, I was scared," she said. "Gills ran the length of her ropey neck. And then, she screamed, and I saw her fangs."

"Why'd she scream?"

She shrugged. "I think it was a scream like we'd scream if we were surprised by a strange animal. Or maybe she was trying to tell me something. She put her hands under my bum, lifted me out of the water, and bolted me toward the shore. I landed and then I coughed up salt water. And none of the other campers ever knew."

"You didn't tell anyone?"

"Oh, honey. At Bible camp? No. I didn't mention it. I did, however, switch my allegiance from Jesus to mermaids. I'd seen something way better than what they were offering at low-rent Jesus camp. And it was right here. On the planet."

She continued. "I couldn't stop thinking about my experience. Nothing could top it. I didn't tell my parents, not yet. I started playing with mermaid dolls, reading about mermaids, dressing like a mermaid little by little. Not the frightening one I saw, but the ones humans love. I wanted to bring joy with my mermaid persona, my mer-sona."

"And the witchcraft?"

"I found witchcraft later. And it worked. This is all real. My nails may be fake, my fins, my tail, my hair color. But when you put it all together and cast a spell or cleanse a space—that's real. As real as you or me."

I looked into those eyes—eyes that'd seen something mystical. I could feel my heart press against my breastbone, like it was trying to get to hers. All I could think was how I wanted to tell her how I'd died once and came back. Let her know about our similar connection.

I stopped myself. Why would she believe me? I didn't have the help of any creature, mythical or otherwise. I'd been knocked over by a hick on a moped. My story was stupid by comparison.

I shook my head to clear it of the urge to tell stories from my life.

"I'm sorry, did you say *tail*?" I asked.

"I did," she said. She shimmied a little, like she was excited. "I'll show you. But we need to do our protection spell for the clinic first."

She got up and opened a locked cabinet.

"Let's take a few of these," she said, gathering up a few empty jars. "Now come over here and help me. Take two jars and I'll take two. And we're going to fill them with all the sharp shit we can find."

"Like nails or whatever?"

"Careful not to cut yourself, but if you do, the blood will make it extra strong."

"What—"

"Don't worry," she said. "No one's getting hurt today."

Fortunately for our project, both the parking lot and sandy shoreline of Lake Longago were replete with nails, screws, broken glass, bottlecaps, discarded pocketknives, corkscrews, and a variety of other tetanus-inducing objects you wouldn't want your toddler to be walking around barefoot in. Our jars were full in a few minutes.

Anemone lined them up on the beach. "A regular land witch would purify these objects with salt. Since I am a mer-witch, we will use sand."

She made a big show of picking up handfuls of sand and filling each one half-way. "Close your eyes," she said. "Take cleansing breaths and think about protecting the clinic from those weirdoes."

I didn't like sitting anywhere with my eyes closed. I also didn't like facing away from the parking lot. But I was trying to make a friend, so I didn't want to make a fuss. Acting like a bother was the quickest way to get sent out back until after dark.

The breathing, though? Nice. Soothing. The lake sparkled as the sun set, and it was like the dark cloud that followed me around parted, if only for a few minutes.

"*So mote it be*," Anemone said.

Her glitter-lined eyes fluttered open. She gazed at the surface of the water.

She was a goddess.

"What now?" I asked.

"You have a choice," she said.

"A choice? You mean a spell's not like a recipe?"

"It's a recipe," she said. "I'd never thought of it way before." She considered this. "But this next part tends to freak people out, so you have a choice. Better to do a weak spell than no spell."

"Do I need to cram my still-beating heart into one of these jars?" I asked.

She laughed. "No. But you do need to pee into it."

"Shut the front door."

"It's true. I do the pee because I am a mer-witch. Since you are a lay person, you may use lake water. We'll infuse some of you into it, though, by pulling a few strands of hair or fingernail clippings."

"For real?"

"For real," she said. "I wasn't joking about the blood, either, but no need to start there." She stood up, pulled down her pants, put one jar between her legs, pissed, and then put the other and continued pissing. Some pee had dribbled down the side of the jar, so she rinsed it off in the lake.

"See? Easy peasy."

I could not conceive of a scenario where I'd be comfortable peeing in a jar in front of Anemone the glamorous mer-witch.

"I'll do the lake water," I said. I yanked out a few strands of hair, put some in each jar, and dipped them into the lake.

"Nice," she said. "Now, hold the jars close to your heart and put some of your energy in there. Fill it with your feelings of protection for the clinic."

I did so. And I felt something. I really did.

Chapter Eight

MY PERSONAL PROTECTION SPELL
  (Say while holding your crown in front of the body of water)

Gods of the oceans, lakes, rivers, and rain,
  protect me from drowning, free me from pain.
  Deliver me to those who long for magic.
  Send me your spirit, make me pelagic.
  For I am Shimmerfish, Mermaid of the Deep,
  On earth to delight, entertain, comfort, and keep.
  So mote it be. —Shimmerfish

We ran out of time after the spellcraft. Anemone wanted to get me back to my car before dark.

"We're not *fin*-ished," she said. "We'll dive in to mermaiding next time. You're gonna love it."

"A hundred mer-cent," I said.

A sleepless night awaited me after that mind-broadening experience with Anemone.

I'd been doing life all wrong.

I used the phone Dr. Birdsong had given me to look up every-thing I could find about mermaiding.

Splish my splash, because Anemone wasn't kidding. Site after site of mermaid clothes, tails, wigs, makeup, and—my new favorite word—*lore.* I found pageants where mer-people could compete to be crowned Monarch of the Sea, Sensational Siren, or Tip of the Tail.

I couldn't believe my eyes. There were mermaids and mer-witches, mermen, plus-sized mer-people, mer-people of every race and ethnicity. Classic mermaids who glided through sun-dappled water with an effortless grace you know they had to work years to perfect. Mermen who rapped about mer-life. Mer-genies who granted wishes.

A spark ignited in my heart.

I stayed up all night watching videos to learn how to pose with a tail. (*Lie on stomach, smize, kick fin up, arch ever so slightly toward it*), the use of 'pirates' as helpers since tailed-up mermaids can't walk on their own and must be lowered into the water, and how to get over your fear of opening your eyes in a pool or tank.

I witnesses transformations. Normal women, getting off work, and running home to slither into their tails for practice at the public pool. No shame. No embarrassment. In fact, other people seemed delighted by observing mermaids frolicking about during their aqua aerobics classes.

And the names! I thought Anemone was beautiful, but then I found Delphine of the Delta, Glittering Pearl, Galasthar of the Sargasso Sea, Mesozoic Merman (who had a dinosaur theme you had to see to believe).

What was not to love about this?

I discovered silicone tails that change color in the sun.

I dared to dream of having a possession so enchanting.

Maybe. One day. If I'd saved some money.

Mer-culture was everything I didn't know I needed. I felt a

wobbly, metallic vibration in my chest I would later identify as yearning. It's a feeling I wasn't well acquainted with yet. I'd never been able to see past my own nose up until now. Now, all I saw was a flash of fin, sparkling jewels, and videos called *Ten Mermaiding Mistakes* and *Live the Mer-Life.*

I was spellbound.

Could I swim like a dolphin through crystal clear waters, or pose primly on a rock, waves splashing all around me, whilst braiding my fine mermaid hair?

I was in hiding, still, so flopping around town like a magical ocean fish was not in my cards. I turned off my phone.

Mermaiding would have to wait.

There was no way for me to join in, not then. But I couldn't stop my dreams. I envisioned myself surrounded by cascading bubbles, blowing kisses to children from a large tank in the middle of a Las Vegas casino. I imagined being fitted for my own perfect tail, and posing on rocky beaches with surf roaring all around me. As I slept, I was surrounded by cool silence, cutting my way through miles of ocean, toward a future filled with magic and the lightness of being buoyed by the all-encompassing power of the sea.

Chapter Nine

"PRO MERMAID TIP: Always smile. Water up your nose? Smile. Cramp in your calves? Smile. Hair dried out and snapping like twigs? Smile. Guy grabbed your scallop bra? Smile. Kid pushes you into the pool before you're ready? Smile. Security guard leers at you? Smile. Smile. Only smile."—Shimmerfish

Anemone and I had hidden the jars thirty paces from the Women's Whole Health building in four directions: north, south, east, and west. I'd tucked one of mine into the base notch of a loblolly and covered it with pine needles. I hid the other behind the dumpster next to the auto body shop next door. If they inadvertently got some protection, fine by me.

"Can you feel the energy?" Anemone asked. "Clinic. Fortified. Good job, witch."

She shook my hand.

She had a strong grip.

It was the summer of my miseducation, and it was off to an exceptional start.

By day, Anemone and I tag-teamed the front desk at Women's Whole Health.

During the evenings and weekends, I became her pirate.

"Avast ye, matey, or whatever," I said the first time I came out in my pirate costume. It wasn't much more than a pair of khakis, a button-down white shirt, a red bandanna, and a mustache drawn on with waterproof eyeliner.

Anemone's tail was silicone, the expensive kind you'd wear when you want to do all those pageants and events I'd learned about. It cost two thousand dollars, which made my jaw drop when she told me, but when you saw it up close…Worth every penny.

It was as if the person who made it reached up into the sky, pulled down the sunset, and wrapped around each scale and fin. Fiery, resplendent orange made up the main color, with shimmering golden streaks throughout. A line of purple ran down the side of the entire tail, giving it definition and texture. And the fluke? The fluke! I'm going to say it looked and moved like one of those fancy goldfish, but that doesn't quite do it justice. The first time I saw her deep-dive into the dreary waters of Lake Longago, I didn't expect much. But she kicked the fluke up out of the water like a whale or dolphin would, and I had to collect myself.

She put those slippery tights with the scale print on first, and then used about a gallon of lube to get herself into her tail. I helped. "I didn't know personal lube came in five-gallon pump jugs." I said to her one evening before her swim.

"It's required," she said with a laugh. "My tail's a bit too tight."

"Ain't it custom made?" I asked.

"You're a great pirate," she said. "The best."

"Happy to be included," I said. "I never seen nothing like this growing up and it's like, wow, you know?"

"You're sheltered, is all," she said. "Now that you're out of your childhood home and adulting like me, you'll learn so much about the world. I became a mer-witch in spite of my parents.

They don't approve of, care for, or find any interest in my lifestyle."

"Knowing Dr. Birdsong, it's hard for me to imagine your parents aren't enthusiastic about your mer-ing," I said. "She's so open and quirky."

"What are you talking about?" Anemone asked.

"Nothing," I said.

Then she sat there in her silicone tail next to the water, no doubt boiling from the combination of sun, silicone, and lube, as she told me a story to haunt me for the rest of my life.

Here's her version.

Anemone was fourteen years-old and wild as a feral hog. She cut school most days to kick around the quarry and drink beer with high school kids. When she deigned to go to class, she pulled fire alarms, started fights, and otherwise made herself *persona non grata* at her small public school.

She described the sound as, "the world caving in, or maybe the Big Bang," when they smashed into her bedroom door with a legit, combat-grade battering ram.

"The door was hollow in the middle, so it blasted into smithereens," she said. "It was also unlocked."

It was three forty-five in the morning.

Anemone peed the bed.

They didn't let her change clothes, grab a coat, take her purse, or say goodbye to her parents, who were too cowardly to wave from the window.

Four strange men who refused to show their faces wrestled her into a van.

"I was wearing a pair of pee-soaked sweats and a tank top. It was thirty degrees. They wouldn't give me a jacket, socks, or shoes. I've never been that cold before and not since. I didn't know where we were going, if they were going to rape me, if they were going to kill me..."

Minutes. Hours. Days. Anemone thinks she may have been drugged. In and out of consciousness, weak, hungry.

When they arrived at the facility, which was a cinder block building not unlike Women's Whole Health but much, much bigger, she was relieved of her befouled clothes and given a body cavity search. She was offered a cold shower which wasn't much more than a hose shot at her by a toothless man in rubber boots who didn't utter a word.

Anemone had no frame of reference for what was happening to her.

Was it jail?

Would she need a lawyer?

"I was there for four years, I think," she said. "Not one person ever told me why."

Her days ran together. Punishing hikes in hundred-degree heat. Food covered in mold. Regular hose-downs, body cavity searches, inspections, and ransacks of their personal areas.

"They'd lead us out to this big field and whack golf balls at us. If we ran, we got tasered. I watched a girl lose four teeth in one day."

"You ever get hit?" I asked.

"They broke my orbital bone," she said. "That's why Dr. Birdsong said I looked different. One millimeter over and it would've smashed my eyeball to jelly."

She'd lost hope.

"I was consumed with death," she told me. "Then, I met Madison."

Madison arrived clueless, terrified, confused, and Anemone took her under her wing.

"Rough shape," Anemone said. "But I could tell. She was something else."

"The pillbillies would rip your head off and shit down your neck," Anemone continued. "Madison was small and scared. So, I started telling her all about mermaids to give her something positive to focus on."

Anemone told Madison her plans for how she was going to get out of there, whatever it was. Buy a school bus. Fix it up like she liked. Then, she was going to drive it all over to mermaid conventions, pageants, classes.

"See? I told her all about it. Now I'm telling you. We grow by listening to others."

"I don't understand," I said. "Is she out there now, doing the same thing? You going to meet up out there or something?"

"Not likely," Anemone said. "She changed."

"But, why?"

Anemone seemed to lose track of herself. "Madison had the *it* factor, too. Smile that lit up rooms. People loved her."

"What do you mean, 'had'?"

She shook her head. "I mean that she changed her mind. She got out before I did. Left without so much as a goodbye. I never heard a peep from anyone about where she went or anything. But she left me this."

Anemone extracted a thick notebook from a drawer and placed it in front of me.

On the front cover, a label with rainbow-colored lettering: *Shimmerfish.*

"That was her mer-name," Anemone said, as I traced the letters with my finger. "Look inside. It's mer-mazing."

And it was. Detailed drawings of the inside of the school bus I was now sitting in. Lists of mer-gatherings all over North America. Practice scripts for when she was in character as Shimmerfish. Daily entries about her exercise regimen to keep her core strong. Lists of things in her life she hoped to manifest.

Shimmerfish came to life on every page. I felt like I knew her.

"This doesn't seem like someone who'd walk away from mermaiding," I said, eyeing the detail on each page. List after list.

Sketches of costume ideas. Diary entries with inspirational quotes, tips, things she'd learned.

Anemone shrugged and closed the book. She found a pen and scribbled out the lettering on the front. "Well, she was taking dictation from me. It's all my ideas. Plus, I told her I thought she could do with a better name than Shimmerfish," she said. "Mermaids are mammals."

"Can't say I've ever thought about it, but I suppose you're right," I said.

I didn't mention that a school bus was fish-related, too. What did it matter?

"Madison said to me, '*I think of how the light catches a flash of tail, and then it's gone. You don't know if you've seen a fish or a mermaid. I like the mystery of it.*' I can't say I agreed, and I told her she could be my pirate until she figured it out. That was always the plan. I'd be the star; she'd be the pirate."

She wrote *Anemone* underneath the crossed-out *Shimmerfish*. She put it back in the drawer.

"I didn't think she'd abandon me," she said. "Can't trust everybody."

"But, do you think she's—"

Anemone cut me off and continued telling me what she wanted me to hear.

It was already ninety degrees when Anemone woke up to the sound of a raid. "I guess someone with a conscience caught wind of what was happening to us all out there."

The girls were all terrified and huddled together in a corner while a SWAT team turned everything over and upside down.

"The sirens were so loud, and the girls were screaming, screaming, screaming," she said. "I can't hear an ambulance without feeling like I need to drop to the floor. I grabbed the book before they herded us all like cattle onto a bus and dropped us off in downtown Alamogordo."

"Where the hell is Alamogordo?"

"New Mexico. Here's the thing. None of us even knew we were in New Mexico."

I understood what she must've felt like. I'd also been through a violent eviction and landed in a place I didn't know. I started to speak but stopped myself.

Anemone and a handful of her co-inmates milled around town for a few hours, dressed in matching clothes that gave them a cultish appearance, until a pastor from a local church asked Anemone what was going on.

"I told that poor woman everything," she said. "By nightfall, the lot of us were sleeping on the floor of the church common room, and all the Christian ladies came out to make themselves feel better by giving us hot dogs."

"How long were you there?" I asked.

"Only as long as it took me to locate the church collection money. I snatched it, hitched a ride to Albuquerque, and found this bus. Bought it off a guy who looked like Jesus with the money I'd stolen from the collection plate."

"Do you steal a lot?" I asked.

Her tone turned sharp. "I've done what I needed to survive."

"I didn't mean anything by it," I said. And I didn't. "Where was Madison?"

"Those days will be behind me as soon as I get my own mermaid career going. And I'm doing this in her honor."

"What if she shows up?"

Anemone didn't break eye contact with me. Her eyes were watery. "That'd be a miracle," she said. Then, "I miss her."

She got up and rifled around through some papers. Pulled out a brochure. Handed it to me.

I read the front page out loud. "St. Germaine Academy for Girls."

"This is where they sent you?"

"Yup," she said. "Those are stock photos. None of those things exist."

"It looks great. Tennis courts. Grassy meadows."

"All made up. It's a reform school run by a bunch of child-raping psychopaths."

"Did your parents know it was like this?"

She shrugged. "I don't care. They moved on."

"I don't understand."

"When I went to their house, it was empty. And I ended up here, in my bus, with you and Dr. Birdsong and the lake."

"Your parents moved without telling you."

She nodded.

"You can't go home because you *really can't go home.*"

She nodded again. Her lower lip trembled.

I went to her and held her as she cried.

I can still hear her sorrowful sobs, full of yearning, every night as I drift off to sleep.

"And get this," she said, after blowing her nose. "St. Germaine was the patron saint of child abuse."

Chapter Ten

BusBoys Renovations
  2324 E. Riverside Drive
  Truth or Consequences, NM 87901
—Business card found in Shimmerfish's book, along with some bank account numbers.

"You ever think about who you want to be, Amy Jay?"

Anemone was laying on her back on a blanket next to the lake. I was sitting up, squinting out over the water, realizing I needed a pair of sunglasses.

I didn't say anything about it, though.

"I guess not," I said. "I never tried to be anything other than whatever this is."

"I don't think you understand what I'm asking," she said, rolling over on her side and propping herself up on her elbow. The bracelets on her wrists made a jangling sound.

"You can be anything you want, Amy Jay," she continued. "The world is big and wide and filled with people, and you don't have to settle for a small life."

"Are you saying I'm not good enough the way I am?" I asked. I wasn't mad about it, I was confused. I'd never been around people who cared if I lived or died, much less whether I was expressing myself. When you're trying to get through the day with your sanity intact, the last thing a person has time to think about is who they want to be.

"I'm not saying that at all," she said. "I like you. You're a diamond in the rough."

"What's that mean?" I asked.

"That means I see potential for greatness in you. I don't think you see it yet, though."

"You talk to Madison like this, too?"

Her face went white. She rolled over onto her back again.

"Never mind," she said. "You're right. You're fine the way you are."

Was I?

"Am I?" I asked.

The words came out edgier than I'd planned. I didn't mean to make her think I was ungrateful. She'd been a good friend, I think. She'd been my only friend. The only person other than my dead momma I'd given more than a passing thought to. And Rutter, of course, but that was because I was worried he'd try to murder me again if he found out I was out here walking around.

Anemone flipped over to face me again, resting her face on her fist. "I'm trying to help," she said. "I see the way you look at me, my bus, my stuff. You're a sponge."

"I'd never seen nothing like it," I said. I was uncomfortable with this realization. I knew I was fangirling on Anemone inside my mind; I didn't know it showed on my face.

I blushed.

"You're smart," she said. "You're quiet, but I see the light in those eyes. You're thinking. You're realizing. You're waking up."

We'd never spent this much time talking about me. I wanted to tell Anemone things, everything, about me. All about my dead momma, who was criminally insane but once told me my light outshined the stars. I wanted to tell her about being dead once and being left for dead once, and about Rutter.

But my throat closed like a vise around the words before I could get them out.

"You don't want more than this?" She asked. "Working at a podunk women's clinic? Getting screamed at by religious weirdos every single day of your life?"

How could I explain to someone like Anemone what this job and this podunk clinic meant to me?I couldn't, so I remained silent.

Shimmerfish fangirled over Anemone, and I fangirled over Anemone.

It seemed like she'd been there forever and would be there forever. Looking back, it's possible she parked her bus outside of Dr. Birdsong's for a few short weeks. Not quite a month. But at the time, she felt eternal.

As if Anemone read my thoughts, she said, "You'll need a makeover. No offense."

"None taken," I said. "Let's do it. I'm all yours."

I knew I wasn't much to look at. When my dead momma had a revolving door in her bedroom, I cultivated a talent for invisibility. Or, at the very least, neutrality.

As I got older, it got harder to hide, though. Ladies, you know what I mean.

I wanted what Anemone had, though. If she could bring something special out of me with a swipe of clippers, sparkly eyeliner, and an on-trend shade of lip gloss, I wanted to see it.

Everything smelled good. I liked the way she stood in front of me, considering my face with a serious look on hers. I basked in her attention for a few hours.

And when we were done, we looked in her mirror.

"Twins," I said. "We could be twins."

"We're more alike than you think," she said.

Chapter Eleven

TOP MERMAID TOWNS:
  Tampa (best, most affordable)
  Orlando (lots of opportunities)
  Miami (CRUISE SHIPS)
  Panama City (redneck riviera)
  Las Vegas (maybe??? Prefer REAL WATER)
  Key West (v. competitive)
  Maui (DREAM!!!!!!)
  Puerto Vallarta (work on your Español, girl!) —Shimmerfish

It wasn't my birthday. Or Christmas. Or any holiday I knew or cared about. When there was a big box all wrapped in pretty paper waiting for me at work, I was confused.

"What's this for?"

Dr. Birdsong and Anemone were bouncing on the balls of their feet and grinning like a couple of Cheshire cats. They reminded me of my dead momma getting giddy over someone else's bad news.

As far as presents go, can't say I've gotten many in my life. I'm not a materialistic person and I don't care much for big emotional displays of affection. But that box, big as a bed pillow, wrapped in shimmering, glittery paper, and topped with an oversized bow, piqued my interest.

"It's for you," Dr. Birdsong said. "Anemone and I agreed we wanted to share our appreciation for all your hard work around here."

"I picked it out myself," Anemone said, her cheeks flushed.

"I don't pretend to understand what you two get up to with all this mermaid stuff," Dr. Birdsong said. "But I've seen you light up since you met Anemone. And I like to support ladies lighting up. Go on. Open it."

I didn't even know what to do.

Anemone pushed the box closer to me. "It ain't gonna bite."

Part of me didn't want to ruin this perfect scene. Something clicked into place for me, right then.

It would be years before I'd feel it again and even longer before I could put a name to it. That day, I felt *belonging*.

Dr. Birdsong and Anemone, by sliding a box across a counter to me, were asking me to be one of them. Someone clean. Someone smart. Someone worthy of gifts.

I should've cried. I was beyond tears; I was in awe.

"You're killing me," Anemone said. "Open it, or I will."

"Doctor's orders," Dr. Birdsong said.

"Do you want to keep the paper?" I asked.

"Oh, for heaven's sake, tear into it," Dr. Birdsong said. "Make a mess."

I did as I was told. The paper came off in a few rips. I put the bow to the side because there was no reason to destroy a perfectly good bow.

I lifted the top off the box, caught the tiniest glimpse of glimmery pink and aqua, and had to step away.

"No," I said. "You didn't."

"Take it out," Anemone said. "I'm dying to see it in person."

I approached the box again and lifted out my new tail.

It unfurled to the floor. It took my breath away.

I'd never owned something so beautiful.

"And a bikini? And a monofin?"

"All yours," Anemone said. "We got you the starter kit."

"This looks better than a starter kit," I said.

"It does," Dr. Birdsong said. "It looks expensive. I mean, it wasn't cheap. But I thought those things would be less, well, cool." She rubbed the fabric between her fingers.

"It's all so cool," I said, still in a state of shock. "Thank you. Thank you so much."

"You're welcome," they said in unison.

"Does this mean you don't want me to pirate for you anymore? You want me to mermaid too?"

"I figured we could help each other," Anemone said. "You'll be a better pirate if you know all about mermaiding." She took my hands in hers. "You're my sea-ster now."

"You two," Dr. Birdsong said, her eyes filling with tears. "Have brought me so much joy. Who knew all this old doctor needed was a stranger from nowhere, a long-lost niece, and four feet of rainbow spandex to feel good again?"

We all laughed, my smile natural and easy.

The day flew by. The protestors made us laugh; the patients gave us purpose. Nothing could go wrong. All was right with the world.

As soon as the clinic closed for the day, Anemone and I shot out of there and headed for the lake.

Chapter Twelve

"Mermaids aren't bigots, mean girls, catty boys, or cliquey snobs. Anyone can be a mermaid, and the mer-community welcomes every shape, size, color, nationality, language, and skill level. Everyone has a little mer in them. It's your job to help them find it."—Shimmerfish

The air was bright and balmy that evening on Lake Longago, and I needed a mermaid name.

"What's it going to be?" Anemone asked as she unfurled my tail onto the sand.

"I haven't much thought about it," I lied. I'd been thinking about it since Anemone said her name was Anemone. "I thought my destiny was pirate, so I'd been thinking of names like *Plank Me, Baby,* and *Barnacle Betty.*"

I was still playing it a bit cool with Anemone. It was probably obvious how out-of-my-gourd twitterpated I was about being a mermaid, but I didn't think I could let on yet.

"Now's your chance," she said. "Off the top of your head."

"How do you feel about Starshell?" I asked.

Her face went blank. "You're telling me you haven't been thinking about mermaid names, and you pull Starshell out of your blowhole? Bullshit, Starshell."

She punched me lightly on the arm and I laughed.

"Busted," I said. "It's good, though?"

"Yeah," she said. "Yeah. It's fin-tastic. Nice to meet you, Starshell."

"Pleased to sea you as shell," I said.

"Okay, you're feeling it. Go get your bikini on and we'll shimmy you into your tail, madame. It's ready for you."

I dipped into the bus to change into the rest of my costume. The starter kit came with a bikini and a crown made of plastic scallop shells.

The bikini was a problem.

I was always taller than the other girls in my class. For some reason I sprouted up and out like I was in a race. Fully developed by the fifth grade; first period in sixth. I'd been a 36D for years. Had to borrow my dead momma's bras.

I did my best to hide my shape from everyone. Figured I'd forever be a baggy T-shirt gal.

I'd made a promise to myself I'd never be humiliated in public ever again. But here I was, staring at a bedazzled bikini top. A gift.

A curse?

I'd begged Momma to let me please, please, please join dance team. With their styled hair, flashy leotards, and covetable moves, my school's dance team was the most glamorous thing I'd seen in my short life.

"I'll earn the fifty dollars myself," I said, breathlessly trying to convince her.

"Won't be necessary," she said. "Rutter, give the girl some cash. She wants to be on dance team."

I didn't understand the smile on her face, but I took the win.

Dance team was my destiny. I could dance! And the daily workout made me feel empowered and focused. The girls were friendly, but distant. I got it. I wasn't one of them. Their mommas took them to competitions in Columbus and Savannah. My momma didn't even pick me up after late practices.

We didn't need to be friends to dance. I lost myself in movement.

First performance. Jazzy number. I was in the back, mostly. Tall.

I was overjoyed to be included.

But there was a problem.

None of the costumes fit me, and we didn't have the time or the money to order a new one from Terri's Tip Tap Toe Costumes & More.

One of the other mothers saw me in my too-tight costume and pulled me aside.

"Sugar, are you comfortable in your costume?"

I nodded, tongue tied, intimidated.

"Let's get you a small cover-up. I think you'll feel better."

She swept out of the cafetorium and came back with what she called a shrug. It was a small sweater that consisted mostly of sleeves, open in the front, with a tiny snap closure.

Covered my heaving bosom, though. I understood what was happening.

I saw the mom chatting with the dance team coach. The shrug was yellow; our costumes were pink. But I watched as the coach decided it was for the best. She never said a word to me but gave me a thumbs up.

Shrug it was.

On the night of the performance, the dancers snuck peeks from behind the curtain to locate their families.

I knew not to bother.

But when the music started, I went away. I could feel the rhythm pulsing through my body. I contorted my face into a wide smile, as I'd been taught. The warm feeling of the theater lights on my skin, the volume of the music, my own movements

—I got swept away to a place where everything was motion, art, presence.

I was having fun.

Tamsin had a history of missing her marks. It wasn't her fault. She had bad eyes and refused to wear glasses on stage.

She spun into me. The sequins from her costume latched onto my shrug with hungry teeth. As she spun back to her spot, the shrug went with her, leaving me exposed.

I could hear tittering in the audience. Block it out, I thought. They could be laughing about anything. It's not you. It's not you.

I'd been yanked out of my orbit and dragged to the cold, unforgiving earth.

There was no saving me.

Tamsin collided with me again, this time in a vigorous turning run.

My left boob popped out of my too-small costume.

The audience gasped.

"Amy Jay?" I heard from the crowd. "More like Amy Double D."

I left the stage.

When Momma asked me how it went, I told her I didn't think dance was for me.

"Amy Jay, people are never going to look at you right. Why give them the chance to put their beliefs on you? Stay in the weeds where you belong."

The realization I'd become a joke felt like swallowing a huge, rigid pill. I choked it down because I had to, and this belief became a part of me. I was a joke from the top of my head to the tip of my toes, throughout my nervous system, in my blood, and within the fibers of my muscles. A big. Fucking. Joke.

But here I stood, looking at a teeny-weeny bikini top, ready to give life another go. I'd fallen inexpressibly in love with mermaiding. And if I was going to mermaid, I needed to put drama behind me.

"You are not a joke," I said to myself. "You are a mermaid."

Fake it 'til you make it, I'd heard someone say once.

There was no way I was going to stand in Amenone's bus naked for longer than a second, so I undressed and re-dressed as fast as I could. I caught a quick glimpse of myself in Anemone's full-length mirror. I took my hair out of its top knot. I put on the scallop crown.

"Starshell," I said.

I stepped out of the bus and made my way toward Anemone. I knew I wouldn't be able to handle it if she laughed at me.

I stood in front of her. Relaxed my shoulders. Waited.

"Starshell," she said, nodding with approval. "You wouldn't know it from your terrible T-shirts and baggy sweats, but Starshell has swagger."

Relief.

"Are those tears?" she asked. "There's no crying in mermaiding. You can't cry underwater."

I laughed at the joke. "I worried, is all."

"Girl, why? You have a banging mermaid bod. You look mermazing."

I wanted to throw myself at her, hug her, engulf her, eat her ears, chew her hair, swallow her whole. I loved Anemone more than anything. Her approval was enough for me to live on.

I shivered, shook it off. I needed to change the subject. Her gaze was too approving.

I took another long look at the tail and marveled over the details. "Look at this fluke." I ran my hand over the bottom part of the tail, where it fanned out into a butterfly's wing in magenta, aqua and sky blue. If you looked closely, you could see tiny scales and bubbles.

"It's sublime," she said. "Your monofin is inside there, so your feet will be all the way at the bottom of the tail. Kick both feet at the same time; use your core. Point those toes. You've seen me do it."

I nodded. I wanted to get in my tail as fast as possible.

I also wanted to run to the hills.

"Come on now," Anemone said. "Let's make this o-fish-ull."

"It's different from your tail," I said, not a complaint.

"Well, yeah. I'm a pro. Mine's made of silicone, and it needs to be if I'm going to win pageants. But you're a beginner. Now stop stalling."

"No lube for me?"

She laughed. "Your lube days are coming. But you won't need it for a non-silicone tail. Let's get you out on your maiden voyage. I'll swim with you."

The tail was tight, and it took both of us yanking and pulling to get the top part up over my belly.

"I'm a sausage," I said. "Fish sausage."

"That's a sea-sage to you," she said.

I laughed.

"You look gorge," she said. "We're gonna come up with a makeup look for you, Starshell. But this tail fits you like, well, a tail. It's good."

"I feel like we should get Dr. Birdsong out here. To see this. It's her gift too." I flopped around a bit, getting into my fishy groove.

Anemone ignored this.

"Can you roll over onto your stomach?"

I did so.

"Strike the pose, Starshell!"

I kicked my legs into an L-shape and my fluke smacked the back of my head. I grinned.

Anemone pretended to snap a photo. "Sexy, Starshell! There's a mermaid in there. I knew it."

I knew it, too. I couldn't wait to meet her.

* * *

"I think I can wiggle myself into the water. I'd hate for you to have to pick me up. You're not my pirate."

Anemone was trying to figure out how to get me in the water. I was so afraid I'd pop out of that costume, too. I wanted her to stop tugging and pulling at me.

She tried a few times before I decided to roll in.

"There's a mermaid scoot," she said, barely able to keep herself from laughing. I didn't mind if she thought it was funny. "I've never seen a roll, but maybe that can be your thing."

The water was cold and clear, and I didn't like how it felt as it whooshed into my tail. Everything got heavy and hard to maneuver while I was still half in the water, so there was no dawdling. I had to submerge myself or I'd be stuck on the shore, a wet, floppy mess.

"Kick! Kick, Starshell!" Anemone called out.

My natural inclination was to scissor kick. No dice. I caught on real fast. I pumped my legs like I'd seen in the mermaid videos, and it worked! But I wasn't in shape to keep it up for long.

Anemone joined me in the water in her swimsuit and monofin and took me through a few standard moves. The forward-moving kick itself was more of a roll—a full-body undulation—and once she demonstrated how I should lead with my hands out in front of me in a sort of prayer position, I had an easier time of it.

"Your abs are going to be sore tomorrow," she said. "I can't wait to show you how to do bubble kisses."

I couldn't either.

We'd been in the lake about an hour when Anemone's teeth started to chatter.

"I need to head in," she said, her lips blue.

I was worn out and I could feel blisters forming on both feet from the repeated flapping of my monofin, but I had fallen head over flippers for mermaiding. I didn't want it to end.

"A few more minutes," I said.

"You shouldn't overdo it," she cautioned. "We can come back out tomorrow."

"Go on in," I said. "One more minute. I promise."

"I wish you wouldn't," she said. Her teeth chattered. Her eyes were fixed over my shoulder. "It's not safe."

"You worried about those guys?" I motioned toward where I thought she was looking. A couple of dudes were hanging out in an inflatable boat.

"Yeah, I am," she said. "Don't go."

I didn't listen. I thought it was kind of her to worry about my safety, but nothing she could have said or done could have made me change my mind.

"Back in a sec," I shouted as I kicked away from her.

I dolphin-swam with enthusiasm to a part of the lake where a few trees had fallen in. My dead momma always dragged our Christmas trees into the lake back home because she swore the fish laid eggs in the submerged branches. I don't know how she knew, and it probably wasn't true. But I wanted to see for myself if other people sank their old Christmas trees into lakes like Momma said they did.

I dove, using my monofin to propel me into the darkest part of the water. I turned around and looked up toward the light breaking through the surface.

It was glorious. And jarring.

I was engulfed by quietude. My thoughts drifted away as I kicked up colder water from the deeper parts of the lake, creating prickly chills over my skin.

I found the trees. Underwater branches were crone's fingers reaching for me, beckoning me closer. I'd never felt more present, or more real. Which is a funny thing to say for a girl in a fish-shaped bathing costume.

Then.

There, in the dark, she was.

I had to stop myself from gasping.

Green-tinged skin, eyes milky, hair the color of mud. A tail, like mine, in shades of grey and brown.

Her mouth was open. One eye seemed to have collapsed on itself. The other open wider than it should have been.

Her hand reached toward me.

I swam closer. Was she calling to me?

Her hair, tinged a mucous shade of yellow, billowed around her face like soft pond rushes; her body pulsated toward me in a macabre dance.

I couldn't look away. I surfaced for a quick suck of oxygen and dove under again, this time using my monofin in one quick thrust to move me toward her.

Branches scratched me as I brushed by, trying to hold my breath long enough to hear from her.

What was she trying to tell me? Her mouth was open, but I heard no sound.

She twisted and undulated in the waves I created under the water.

The sun went behind a cloud, and the lake was plunged into darkness.

I lost sight of her.

One more breath.

I dove as fast as I could, eyes burning, core on fire, only to be confronted with darkness, cold, and silence.

Did I see what I thought I saw?

I surfaced and began kicking toward the shore.

"Anemone!" I called.

But she'd already left the water.

Chapter Thirteen

"Face your fears. Remember when you couldn't open your eyes underwater? Or when you hyperventilated at the thought of holding your breath? You're holding your breath for three minutes now. Swim forward. Keep pushing."—Shimmerfish

I'd imagined it. Her.

Mer.

I wanted to be like Anemone. To be drowning and saved rather than chased on land and forced into hiding under an invasive bush crawling with insects. I craved a magical experience, one with a memory I could carry for the rest of my days in case my situation never improved.

Who wouldn't want to spot a mermaid underwater? The mind plays tricks.

It was better not to mention what I saw. Good chance Anemone would accuse me of copying her.

Wasn't work the risk.

I was transforming.

Not only was I learning dolphin kicks, how to float, how to sink, and even more advanced moves like figure eights, but Anemone showed me how to apply waterproof makeup, false eyelashes—the works.

Everything was challenging. According to Anemone, learning in a lake was more difficult than learning in a pool.

"I'll take burning chlorine eyes over whatever brain amoebas are out here," she said once. "But the lake's all we have. Unless you want to start breaking into the country club out Route 2."

I didn't. And I didn't know the difference, so to me, these evenings and weekends in the lake were ideal.

Sunkissed, bleary-eyed, and aching through my core, I'd spend evenings on the bus flipping through Shimmerfish's book.

Every page, a marvel. Shimmerfish had created collages, mood boards, makeup strategies. She had a calendar with deadlines for mermaid competitions and workout plans. She even had budget breakdowns for purchasing the bus, sketches for the renovation, and magazine and newspaper clippings filled with tips and tricks for living on the road.

I took all of it to heart. Shimmerfish made a life as a professional mermaid seem possible.

She made it seem magical.

Shimmerfish had her shit together.

Anemone insisted she was the driving force behind all of the information in the book, and Shimmerfish was the one who wrote it all down.

"Her handwriting was neater than mine," Anemone said.

Her assertions fell flat with me. I'd been on the bus every day for weeks now, and none of the meticulous attention in the Shimmerfish book matched Anemone's behavior. At all.

Anemone was a slob. She'd drape her priceless, custom mer-tail over the table to dry or left it on the floor, still covered with sand. Her makeup kit was in shambles, with broken compacts, colors smashed together, and misshapen lipsticks. Food wrappers, every-where. Even in her bed.

My dead momma used to eat in bed. The thought of it made me gag.

Anemone didn't manage the bus well either, which was even more concerning. The steering wheel would pop off (never while she was driving, thank heavens, but it came off when we were parked). Strange black smoke billowed from underneath the hood.

After our lessons and sessions, I'd tidy up while she watched.

Nothing matched up.

But I didn't care.

I was living in my body in a new way. I luxuriated in my sore muscles, stinging eyes, and ears full of lake water. I didn't mind when tiny bits of glitter collected in the corners of everything or when my crown got so tangled in my hair we'd have to cut it out.

I skipped to work in the morning and skipped out the minute it ended.

"Only twelve bomb threats this morning, Doctor," I said in a chirpy tone the morning after Anemone and I had finalized my Starshell look. Starshell was hot pink lips, long lashes, a splash of scallop shells over my eyebrow—all plastered in place with toxic amounts of some kind of sticky setting spray. I loved it.

I delivered the news with pep and optimism. Because of mermaiding, I was in the best shape of my life, sleeping great, feeling refreshed. Nothing, not even a bomb threat, could sour my mer-mood.

"High? Or low?" Anemone asked, the edges of her lips bent into a frown.

"It's up," Dr. Birdsong said.

"Most we've had in a while," I agreed.

"Wonder what's got their panties in a bunch all of a sudden," the doctor said, peering out the window.

"I'm going to find out," Anemone said.

The wind she created as she stormed toward the door lifted my bangs. She was out before she could be stopped.

I dashed to the doorway to try to stop her, but it was too late.

"Hey, you all. Yeah, you. It's a federal offense to leave threatening messages for people."

"Whore!"

"Your mama's a whore," Anemone said in a tone that made me believe the man's mama might be a real whore. "She should've aborted you."

The crowd pressed toward the building, sweeping Anemone backward. I grabbed her the moment she reached the doorway and pulled her around the reception desk to safety.

They were coming in.

The energy shifted and the ugly, snorting mob was in the building.

Seconds.

Every bit of glass, shattered. Bottles of pills, stolen. Furniture ripped to shreds or thrown into the parking lot.

The sound of Dr. Birdsong's panicked screaming still haunts me. She stumbled toward the desk phone, but she was too late. Someone had pulled the cord.

Anemone was in her element. She threw punches, pulled hair. Kicked one guy in the groin before another one had grabbed her by the hair and dragged her outside.

They pissed on everything.

Dr. Birdsong had given up on calling for help and was ferrying the patients out the back exit.

Anemone came roaring back, holding two of the spell jars in her hand. She lobbed them into the melee, and they shattered. Shrapnel and piss shot out, but only added to the mess.

"Get out, Starshell!" she shouted above the din. "Call the cops!"

I hadn't realized I was standing in the corner dumb as a mannequin until I heard Anemone call my name.

I shuddered the way I'd seen people do after they'd been saved from drowning.

Arms, elbows, knees were everywhere.

And a smell.

It wasn't piss or blood or fear.

It was pemmican made of game meat. Stale Coors. Winstons.

My stomach churned.

Any one of them could be him.

I darted out the back. The doctor was on the phone, explaining the situation to the dispatcher.

The police pulled in. Lights, no sirens. One of them appeared to be finishing up a phone call. They sauntered over to the scene.

As the crowd dispersed in the parking lot, I scanned faces for anyone who might be Rutter.

First, I hallucinated mermaid. Now, I was getting real paranoid about Rutter

Was my mind playing tricks on me? Or was that his smell?

The police had arrived in time to stop a guy from setting the whole building on fire, but you could tell they wanted him to do it.

No one was on our side.

An hour later, after the police had arrested precisely no one and didn't even write down our witness statements, the three of us stood surveying the wreckage.

I kept looking over my shoulder.

Was he still out there?

"They're gone, Amy Jay," Anemone said. "Calm down."

I winced. She didn't call me Starshell.

"Glad no one was injured," Dr. Birdsong said. "Anemone, I've got to say I'm surprised at you."

"What do you mean?"

"I've never seen you behave with such disrespect. To anyone. You were always well-mannered with adults. When you were eight."

Anemone's mouth was a straight line. Her eyes lost their

brightness and took on a cruel, dull expression. Her neck was an angry red shade where a member of the violent mob had tried to choke her.

"How the fuck would you know?" she asked, her eyes fixed on what remained of the clinic.

"Phoebe Birdsong," Dr. Birdsong said, her words more pointed than her tone. "What's become of you?"

"Shit's changed," Anemone said. She popped her knuckles. She licked her lips. "Not like any of y'all were paying attention."

I watched them both. They didn't look at each other or acknowledge Anemone's rudeness. It pained me to see Dr. Birdsong turn white, her tongue tied, her heart broken.

"You girls go on," Dr. Birdsong said, her voice a whisper. "I'll lock up what's left. We'll convene tomorrow to clean everything up. Amy Jay, you can call around in the morning and let everyone know their appointments are canceled for the foreseeable future."

I wanted to stay with Dr. Birdsong. To do whatever it took to undo this.

Why was destroying things so easy for people? What made adults behave like animals?

Why couldn't everyone take a mer-pill and chill out?

"Dr. Birdsong—" I began.

"Don't," she said. "This isn't your fault, Amy Jay. No one is to blame. Go. I'll see you both tomorrow."

My shoulders slumped as exhaustion surged through my bones. Anemone walked differently, too. Her back was straighter. Her neck, stiffer. Her jaw tightened in a way that made her appear aggressive, spoiling for a fight.

She'd transformed into something I didn't recognize.

We tiptoed through the wreckage. Anemone opened the door to her bus and climbed in.

"You coming? It's not even noon. We got a whole day to swim."

What could I do but climb in?

Chapter Fourteen

When You Arrive In Tampa (Or Wherever)
   •Find a mer-pod asap.
   •That's it. That's the note.
   •This is happening! —Shimmerfish

Anemone and I motored out to the lake.

One of the longest drives of my life.

Witnessing the destruction of the place that had been my safe haven had left me speechless. I couldn't stop seeing the look on Dr. Birdsong's face. She'd been a wacko, but a sweet, loving wacko who'd weathered death threats and insults, and now a violent mob. And Anemone was acting like it wasn't her fault.

Rutter's smell clung to me, a bad omen.

It was Anemone's fault.

Dr. Birdsong and I had a balance. We'd learned how to manage the zealots without endangering the important medical work we were doing at the clinic. We kept our integrity, in a way.

Who did Anemone think she was? In my mind, she wasn't no

more than a drifter who caused problems for people I cared about. I'd built a life here, and she had to go out and start a world war.

The shine was off.

Anemone was selfish.

Or should I say, *shellfish*, I thought.

And I was right burned out by selfish people who do whatever they want without a thought to the consequences.

I clicked my jaw.

"Today was a lot," she said.

"Sure was," I said. "You told them."

She smiled. "I guess I did. Right on time, too."

"What do you mean?"

"I'm outta here tomorrow."

Was the snap audible? I heard a loud pop. The person I was before Anemone said that, and the person I was after she said that, were two different beings.

It was time for her to go, she said. No plans to help clean up the mess she created.

I seethed. The skin on my neck crackled as it erupted into angry, crimson hives. My throat swelled, refusing to allow me to say what I wanted to say.

I'd never been angry before. My body was in revolt.

I started to put some things together on the drive, in the spotlight of Anemone's outburst. Things I'd willfully ignored or rationalized away.

I had questions.

Everything about Anemone made me want more out of life. More glitter and sparkles. More glamor. More friends.

But Anemone didn't value anything she'd built.

I didn't notice at first, having been ensorcelled by Anemone's whole schtick. But now all I could see were chip bags, empty cans of this and that, along with stacks of unopened mail addressed to her, littering every surface. Had the windows always been this grimy? The chassis, this bug-splattered? Her bracelets and necklaces were often clumped together in impossible knots.

Her tail was in a heap on the floor again.

Looking at this disorder, I thought about two things. One, if I had such fine items, items I'd worked hard on and paid for with stolen money, I'd cherish them.

Two, Anemone's outer cool may be a front. I read in one of our waiting room magazines that the vibe in your space is a reflection of what's happening inside. Like, with your emotions.

You could look at my space and think I had nothing going on inside. I hoped my space reflected my financial situation rather than my emotional situation, but the article had a point. I was empty. Had been for a while.

Was Anemone a mess inside?

Maybe so, but I'd wanted to be like her anyway. What a gorgeous, radiant, complicated mess she was. I thought I might like someone to think the same about me one day. I'd like to look people in the eye and tell them about my life. I'd like for people to find me an intriguing mystery. I'd like to have the freedom to move anywhere, anytime, far away from Rutter. Far away from myself.

Could you forget the past by driving away from it, becoming someone new? Or do your fears, traumas, and difficulties come along with you?

Baggage, I thought wryly. Sure, I could pack up and go with Anemone (not like she'd asked me). But wouldn't I still be who I was?

Anemone was agitated but was pretending like she wasn't. I'd seen this behavior before when my dead momma was trying to convince me I hadn't seen one of her stephusbands crush her hands between his. Or when she tried to sweet-talk bill collectors.

"I think we should go for a swim," she said. "We'll work on side dolphin kicks."

I couldn't look at her. I wanted to get out, to run home.

But what if Rutter was there?

"Not tonight," I said. "Today was a lot. I want to go home."

I started picking up trash and collecting it into one of the many empty bags lying around.

"Stop," Anemone said.

"Stop what?" I crumpled up some Luna bar wrappers and put them in the bag.

"Stop cleaning."

"If I didn't clean, you'd be living like a hog," I said. "Maybe you do need a pirate. Heck, maybe you should be my pirate. I care about all this more than you do." I kicked her tail out of the way with my foot.

Anemone didn't say a word. She sat down in the driver's seat. Started the engine and drove me home.

She opened the bus door without saying a word.

I gritted my teeth and stepped onto the street without saying goodbye.

I ran to my front door, the smell of pemmican, stale Coors and Winstons amplifying with every step.

The bus groaned as Anemone put it into gear.

I shoved my key into the lock, but I was too afraid to go in. The smell was overpowering.

Was Rutter inside?

I heard the bus pull away.

I froze.

Fear sliced through me like a machete.

The bus stopped at a light two blocks away.

I ran, fast as I could, my blood throbbing in my ears.

Banged on the back of the bus.

The doors folded open.

Anemone shot me a smug smile as I climbed aboard.

"Ready for a swim?" she asked without taking her eyes off the road.

"Drive," I said. "I've got some stuff to tell you."

Chapter Fifteen

"Don't be afraid to ask for help or to rely on your sea-sters for assistance. You're good at underwater tricks and poses; another mermaid may be better at makeup, facial expressions, and sourcing costume stuff cheap. Everyone has a different skill (krill?) set. Celebrate it."—Shimmerfish

Rutter was in town, and I cracked like an egg. My story came pouring out of me like a levee broke.

"Don't tell Dr. Birdsong," I said to Anemone through sobs, in conclusion.

Anemone was pacing and grinding her teeth. I could see her jaw muscle working overtime. She stopped and pointed at me.

"That's fucked up, Amy Jay. Fucked. Up."

I was talked out. Had enough. I was limp as a rag doll, tired as a miner.

"This Rutter character is still out there? And you think he found you?"

I nodded.

"And you're not making this up? It's real? The umbrella pole and everything?"

I nodded.

She continued her pacing. She mumbled under her breath. I willed myself to shrink, to disappear.

"You have to go to the police," she said. "You have to. He's going to kill you."

I started to shake. My mouth went sour.

"I can't," I whispered.

"I can't either," Anemone said. "I can't be around authority after what happened to me. But you. You need to go. File a report. Get this motherfucker off the streets."

"I can't," I said a little louder.

"You need to at least tell Dr. Birdsong."

"I can't," I said again.

"You must. We're going to her house right now."

"Please don't," I said.

"But why?"

"Anemone, I'm..."

"What, Amy Jay? What are you?"

"I'm sixteen."

She sat down. She looked away.

"You're telling me you hid from a man named Rutter, stole money he thought was his, escaped in a stolen car you weren't licensed to drive, and now you're hiding out? And he's in town?"

"Sums it up," I said.

I wanted to hide from her, to cover my shame.

I got up and paced the bus. My nerves jangled, like someone had let a chainsaw rip somewhere in my torso.

"Are we still friends?" I asked her. I surprised myself with this question. Moments ago, I'd been willing to walk away from her, from all of it, because she was mean. Now, all I wanted was to curl up in her lap and have her stroke my hair.

"Are you serious?"

"Yes," I said. "I'm sorry to have dropped this on you like a cat leaving a dead rat on your doorstep."

"That what you think?" she asked. "We can't be friends because of what happened—of what's happening—to you?"

I shrugged. I looked at my feet.

She came over and took both my hands in hers.

"Of course we're still friends," she said. "And as your friend, I'm going to take care of this for you. Tonight."

* * *

"You've seen protection magic already," Anemone said. She'd pulled the Shimmerfish book out and was flipping through some pages at the end. "We're going to do a spell to wrap you in safety, and then we'll do a hex."

"A hex?"

"Yes," she said. "When I was working with Madison—Shimmerfish—I was adamant we only do white magic. We're going to need to go dark on this one, I'm afraid."

"What's the difference?" I asked.

"Exactly what you'd think," she said. "The spells I do are to bring good things, support someone, help them attract abundance. A hex is designed to harm. But it's called for in this case."

"As long as it doesn't harm us, I guess," I said. I was fascinated by her gathering of items. A white candle. A black candle. Small slips of paper. Some pretty stones.

"That's the thing," she said, shoving the trash on the table to the floor and motioning for me to take a seat. "Hexes can boomerang."

"How?"

"It means they'll come back around and hit you with up to three times the strength. Don't worry, though. It's necessary in this case. He tried to kill you. If that's not his own hex, then I don't know what is. Do you have a photo of him?"

I shot her a look. "Of course not," I said. "Are you saying his attempt to kill me could be seen as a hex? And our hex is his hex boomeranging on him?"

"Yes," she said. "You're going to make a very powerful mer-witch one day."

I couldn't have beamed more if she had booped me on the nose. I wanted that. I wanted to be a powerful witch. Or mer-witch. Or anything, really.

All friends have disagreements, right? I could feel myself forgiving her for everything as the minutes ticked by.

We were friends. Sea-sters. Mer-witches in arms.

Anemone could be messy. Life was messy.

She handed me the white votive and a needle and told me to scratch my name in it. I did so. I put the candle down on the table between us.

As Anemone lit the candle, she explained I was to focus on the flickering flame, imagine myself wrapped in pure white light with a black border around it, and ask out loud for protection.

She lit the candle, and I stared into it.

"What am I supposed to say? Are there words or a poem or something?"

"Ask for what you want in plain language," she said. "No need to get fancy unless you want to."

The flickering of the flame had a soporific effect on my mind. It was an alert drowsiness. My focus was strong. My intention was clear.

"Protect me from Rutter and his abuses," I said.

I said it over and over and over until I lost track of time and the candle burned to the bottom.

Anemone was transfixed, and she didn't speak. I'd never felt closer to another person in my whole life.

"*So mote it be,*" she said, taking my hands in hers.

"*So mote it be,*" I repeated.

Her eyes flickered as if she was awakening from a trance.

"What now?" I asked.

"Hex time," she said. "Second verse similar to first. Scratch his whole name into the black votive."

"I don't know his full name," I said.

This had to work. I didn't have a plan B.

"Relax," she said. "It's good to have a photo or the name to help you focus. But, most importantly, you'll concentrate on your intention. That's where the real power is. Are you ready to begin?"

I was. I scratched his name into the candle with the needle.

She lit the candle, and I focused on my intention. Turns out my intention was dark.

"I want Rutter to leave me alone forever." I repeated it a few times, for good measure.

The look on Anemone's face registered her approval. And when we I was done, she said, "*So mote it be.*"

She nodded. I nodded.

"Powerful magic."

"*So mote it be,*" I said. "*So mote it be.*"

Chapter Sixteen

"HOW TO HANDLE HATERS

No one hates you and no one hates mermaids. Those that mock you don't understand how hard you work, the sacrifices you've made. Swim harder. Smile more. They want to be you. Everyone wants to be you." —Shimmerfish

Despite every muscle in my body quaking with fear, we went to my place.

I couldn't wait for Anemone to tell Rutter to fuck all the way off forever.

I opened the door. I scanned the room.

Empty.

I motioned for Anemone to enter.

"This is not where you live," she said, looking around with a pinched face. "This can't be where you live."

She'd never been inside.

I knew it was nothing fancy. But the tone in her voice made me embarrassed about it.

"It's where I live," I said. "What did you expect? I'm poor."

"The world's a hard place," she said, airily. She ran a finger along my kitchen counter. "Nobody hands you anything. You've got to take it. That's what you did."

A compliment. I blushed.

"You and your aunt are the only two people in the world who've seen anything worth anything in me," I said.

"My aunt?"

"Dr. Birdsong."

"Oh, right," she said. "My aunt's been good to you. Does she know you live like this?"

I wasn't sure how much I should disclose about the arrangement Dr. Birdsong and I had about the apartment. It wasn't the time or the place, so I kept quiet.

"Uh-huh." She stood motionless, but I could see the wheels turning inside her head.

She shook her shoulders.

"You ready for what's next?"

I nodded. I could only imagine what she was going to say to him. Anemone had a cutting way with words, and she looked like someone who took no shit. I was a thousand percent confident she would do what it took to get him to leave me alone.

"Here's how this is going to work," she said. "You're gonna be in here, waiting. You're bait."

There was a mer-joke in there, but now wasn't the time. "Yes," I said.

"Good. When he comes, which he will, I want you to open the door."

Terror gripped me but I loved every minute of this. I'd always wanted a friend to scheme with. My dead momma and I would scheme some, but it was usually me doing whatever she wanted, like creating a diversion while she stole stuff.

"What are you going to do?"

I couldn't wait to hear what she had planned.

"You'll see," she said.

She left me in the apartment, alone, and said she was going to hide outside, and wait for him to come by. "Do some chanting and visualizing," I believe she said. "We want an element of surprise. Lure him in. Then I'll do my thing."

I sat in the middle of the room, lights on, palms sweating. Without Anemone's bravado, I realized I was a small person, sitting in a room waiting for a man who wanted me dead.

My breath felt heavy.

Could I trust Anemone?

Doubts pummeled me from every angle. Did she set me up? Was she out there contacting Child Protective Services, or worse, her aunt?

My neck itched. I needed to move.

I got up and walked circles around the empty room. Time moved like molasses.

I was already on the verge of tears. I felt exactly the way I felt the weekend my dead momma and Rutter were supposed to get back from Myrtle Beach. No one called me, told me what was happening. I waited for five extra days until Rutter arrived at the house, unshaven, smelling like himself. He couldn't wait to tell me what'd happened, took a perverse pleasure in describing it to me, told me my dead momma handled her impaling like a champ.

Waiting made me anxious and angry.

I texted Anemone.

> Me: I don't like this. Let's run. I don't want to do this.

> Her: Stay the course.

> Me: I'm scared. And annoyed.

> Her: Shh. I think I see him.

Then, a simple knock on the door. A menacing *shave and a haircut, two bits.*

"Who is it?" I croaked out, my head leaning on the door.

"Open up, Darlin'," Rutter said. "It's your dear daddy."

"You're not my daddy," I said. "What do you want?"

"I think you and I both know what I want," he said. "You can hand the money through the door. Then I'll be on my way, never to bother you again. If you can keep your mouth shut."

This was a good deal, I thought. If all he wanted was the wad of cash I'd taken, I could simply give it to him, and all would be done.

I needed the money, but how much was it worth to be rid of him forever?

Priceless, I thought. If this was how spells worked, then count me in forever.

I willed Anemone not to show up.

I could handle this on my own. Then, she and I could forget all about Rutter. Fix the clinic. Convince her to stay—or for her to take me with her.

"Wait right there," I said.

The money was tucked into the freezer section of my tiny fridge. I grabbed it and hurried back to the door. I didn't want to prolong this transaction.

"I've got it," I said. "I'm opening the door now."

I unlocked the door and opened it as narrowly as I could while sliding the money through.

He snatched it out of my hands.

Before I could close and re-lock the door, he'd muscled his way through. The force was so strong I landed on my butt.

"There's a bit missing, no?"

"I—I needed rent money," I said.

"For this dump?" He took a step closer to me.

"You left me for dead," I said. "If it was up to you, I'd still be out in the woods living on crickets and morning dew."

"If it was up to me, you'd be roadkill," he said.

He fixed his enraged gaze on me and took another step

forward. "You're gonna repay me every dollar you owe me, you understand?" He poked me in the shoulder. "I know where you work. Or where you used to work. I know where you live. I know everything there is to know about you, little girl."

Where was Anemone? This was not how the spell was supposed to go.

"That wasn't our deal," I said. "You said you wanted the money, and you'd go away. You got what's left. I didn't spend it all. Now go."

I attempted to look over his shoulder for Anemone.

"Ain't no one coming to save you," he said. "Why don't you come with me?"

"I don't want to come with you," I said. There was a wild look in his eye. I'd seen it before.

"You don't have a choice."

Where was Anemone?

I scooted away from him as best I could. He strode toward me, grabbed me by my hair and lifted me off the floor.

"Everyone thinks you're off living with family," he said. "No one gives a shit about Amy Jay. It'd be better if you were gone, though. Keep it clean."

Everyone? I thought. *Who's everyone?*

The pain in my scalp was sharp as he yanked and twisted me toward the door. I thought about what they said in school about a second location and realized Anemone was going to need more than a sharp wit to help me out of this fuckery.

We struggled, but Rutter's grip was what my dead momma called white trash strength, and there wasn't much more I could do but hang there and swing at him. I was twisting around so much I feared my scalp would peel away from my skull.

"Hold still," he said through gritted teeth.

I would do no such thing. If he was able to drag me out, he wouldn't be so bone-headed again. He'd kill me for sure. I wasn't going to make it easy on him.

"Anemone!" I called as loud as I could.

Rutter shoved me to the floor. He stood over me and pointed at my face.

"That your safe word? *An enemy*? You got someone hiding here, girl?"

He dragged me around the room. Pulled the bathroom curtain. Searched the empty cabinets.

"You fucking with me?"

"No," I croaked.

"Who's *an enemy*?"

Anemone slipped in the doorway behind him. I didn't dare look at her. She was holding something in her right hand.

"I don't know," I said.

"I'm Anemone," she said.

As Rutter turned to face her, she reared back and let a swing loose. Whatever she was holding took Rutter out in one swift motion. He landed with a thud on the concrete next to me.

I scrambled toward the door.

"Let's go," I said. "You got him. Let's go."

Anemone didn't even turn around. She was holding her steering wheel in her hand.

She straddled Rutter, held the steering wheel to his head, grabbed him by the hair and forced his head through it with so much strength, I thought his nose might break. The wheel was hanging around his neck, and I couldn't see how she was ever going to get it off him. I wondered how he would explain this. I wondered how we were going to drive out of there without a steering wheel.

"Let's go," I said. I didn't like what I was seeing. I'd signed up for a sassy mouthed friend telling Rutter off for being inappropriate with me and him being so humiliated he'd disappear.

I didn't ask for this.

Anemone gripped the steering wheel with both hands. With an assured, purposeful twist, she broke his neck.

The sound of the bones and ligaments snapping sent a powerful wave of nausea through me.

His body slumped to the floor.

I watched Rutter twitch until he stopped.

Anemone stood up. Wiped her nose with the heel of her hand. She wrenched the steering wheel from off Rutter's neck and head, and, from the sound of it, this time she did break his nose.

She took a step toward me. Then, she remembered, and went back to fetch the wad of cash from Rutter's front pocket.

"Now we can go," she said, wiping her hand across her sweaty forehead. "Now we can go."

Chapter Seventeen

I wasn't unaccustomed to violence.

But I hadn't seen such violence toward another person as long as I'd lived.

It was always directed at me.

The visual of Rutter's head contorting in an unnatural motion gripped me like a half-full tick. I couldn't shake it.

More disturbing was the look in Anemone's eyes. It was a continuation of the Anemone I'd seen that morning, wild with rage, determined, frightening. Gone were her soft, feminine edges. She moved like a death machine.

She clicked the steering wheel back into its spot and secured it with the confidence of a professional mechanic.

Was there anything this woman couldn't do?

After an eternity of driving in silence, I spoke.

"Was that what the magic was all about? Did we cause that?"

"Magic? No. That asshole was going to kill you. Wasn't magic. That was me." The words shot out of her like an assault rifle. She was so sure.

A tsunami of shame washed over me. I messed up the spell. I wasn't special. I had no skills, no connection to the divine. I was being hunted by an ignorant redneck because I was an ignorant redneck. I'd be dead if it weren't for Anemone. And her broken steering wheel.

I couldn't stop the tears. I tried not to show Anemone my face as the dam burst.

"You're going to have to leave," she said.

"What? Why?"

Tears turned to panic. Which turned to tight breathing.

She maneuvered the bus into its usual location at the lake. She turned to face me.

"There's a dead guy in your apartment right now," she said. "No one knows me. Your landlady knows you. I reckon you've got about twelve hours before the body starts to reek. You need to get the fuck out of here. Right now."

Since I hadn't planned on there being any killing, it never occurred to me I needed to sort out the next steps.

I had nowhere to go.

My car was at the clinic.

I couldn't leave if I'd wanted to.

"Can we—" I began. "Can I come with you? Be a mermaid with you? I'll pirate, I don't care. I want to come. With you." I was making a spectacle of myself, but I was desperate.

Anemone chewed her lower lip.

"There was a time when I thought I'd ask you," she said. "To come along. I like you, Amy Jay. You're a good egg."

"But?" A teardrop of sweat snaked down my back.

She had a look on her face like the one my school counselor had when I told her I hoped to go to college one day.

"You're a minor," she said. "I can't take you across state lines. I was already locked up once in my life. And love you as much as I do, I'll never risk my freedom again. You need to run, and you need to run on your own."

I was a pile of ashes.

Anemone made a motion toward the built-in banquette. "You can sleep here tonight," she said. "You're exhausted. But first light, I'm taking you to the clinic and you're getting in your dead momma's car and leaving town. Do you hear me?"

I heard her.

Loud and clear.

No sleep welcomed me. I laid there on a hard, scratchy cushion, shoving snack chip packets and random plastic necklaces out of my way, sweating, concocting the barest shred of a plan.

I thought about Anemone. I didn't know her. It's one thing to be a scrappy drifter with a chip on your shoulder; it's quite another to be a person who can shove someone's head through a steering wheel and yank.

I cringed at the memory.

I hated everything about Rutter. But I couldn't gin up enough rage to want him dead. I didn't see what good it would do.

I was right. Because now I was on the run again on account of him. I'd given him the money. What more would he want with me? I hadn't snitched on his other behaviors. No reason to do so now.

There was no un-ringing this bell.

And now Anemone's talking about ditching me. She blew up my life and was about to porpoise off into the warm, welcoming waves and water parks of Florida while I—what? Where the hell was I supposed to go?

It wasn't first light when Anemone woke up. I know because I saw the sunrise myself.

She saw me through swollen eyes. I watched as she remembered the things that'd happened the night before.

"Right," she said. She flopped back onto her pillow.

"I need the money," I said.

"What money?"

"The money Rutter tried to kill me for. You took it. I need it back."

My dead momma once had a dog named Hulk Hogan. Hulk was a pittie the size, shape, and color of a gargoyle. He was smart as a kindergartner and stubborn as an ox. When you asked him to do something he didn't want to do, he'd ignore you. He'd scratch his ear. Look around. Sniff something. As if you weren't standing right there telling him to *drop the bunny* or *get off the coffee table*.

Asking Anemone for my money was like negotiating with Hulk Hogan.

"You want some coffee?" she asked.

"No. I want my money. And then I want you to take me to get my car."

"How about a power bar? You must be starving."

"Anemone."

"I can't let you go until I see you eat."

"I'm not doing nothing until you give me my money back."

Tiny breath in. Tiny breath out. I could feel the familiar itch of hives pulse on my torso.

"One bite," she said.

I realized she had no plans to return my money. I may have been young, but I'd seen some shit in my days, and I knew now there wasn't no trusting Anemone. She was a thief. And a murderer.

I snatched the bus keys and made a break for it.

She chased me off the bus to the edge of the water.

"You'd better give me those fucking keys," she said. "Now."

"Happy to," I said. "When you give me my money."

"You've seen what I'm capable of. And you're half his size. Except for your boobs."

Rude.

I tossed the keys up in the air a few times. "Be a shame if they ended up in the lake."

She took a step toward me.

I took a step into the water.

I continued to toss the keys. Up and down. Up and down.

"This is an easy fix," I said to her. "I don't want to do this. I only want what's mine."

The water lapped against my ankles.

I went a little deeper.

"Amy Jay," Anemone said, her face twisted into a terrified expression. "Don't move."

I didn't feel like listening, so I inched backward a tiny bit.

"Like this?" I did a little wiggle dance. "Shell we dance? Don't clam up, *Phoebe*."

She winced at the name.

Two could play this game. What would Hulk Hogan do?

I yawned. Took another step back. Scratched my ear.

"Stop, Starshell," she said, both hands out in front of her.

I backed into something cold. Rubbery.

Startled, I flipped around to see what it was.

A mangled hand, wet and filmy gray, like it was dipped in wax. A shoulder with a yellow spaghetti strap. Hair the color of mud, with sticks, leaves, and debris tangled in it.

A fluke peeked up from the water a few feet behind her. Gold. With blue striations.

It moved. I squinted to get a better look.

The tail was covered with tiny snails munching on algae growth.

A crab skibbled across a broad, bloated back.

I screamed and bolted from the water.

Anemone was on her knees. Her hands over her mouth. She was screaming with no sound. Rocking.

I kneeled next to her and watched the corpse as it bobbed in the shallows.

"It's a mermaid," I whispered. "A real mermaid."

I started to tell her about how I'd seen her out there in the submerged branches, but the look on Anemone's face let me know now was not the time to start talking.

She took her hand off her mouth. Her eyes were wide with disbelief. She looked at me. She looked at the body.

"That," she began before her sobs overtook her. "Is Shimmerfish."

Chapter Eighteen

THINGS I'VE LEARNED ABOUT MERMAIDING

(for future book???)

•Mermaiding won't make you happy. Making others happy makes you happy.

•Mermaiding might not pay the bills (it might!), but it fills your soul.

•Silicone tails are totally worth it, even if you have to steal from a church to get one.

•Cooling eye gel is a must.

•Men will be gross with you. Smile anyway.

•Not all waterproof mascaras are the same.

•Be more careful about who you take under your wing. Mermaiding is for everyone, but not all mers are a match.

Trying to hold on to happiness was like trying to hold water in your closed fist. I'd tried to have a tight grip on my own happiness that summer, correctly believing it was too good to be true.

When I first met Anemone, happiness was a thunderbolt.

When she and Dr. Birdsong presented me with a mermaid tail? Something hard in my heart softened and a tiny bit of joy wriggled in.

It had been a summer of splashing in the water as the sun went down. I floated, my cares and worries washing away in the dingy water of Lake Longago. I learned how to prevent blisters and keep my eyes open underwater. My lung capacity increased.

Anemone was a wonder in the water. Fast and agile. I longed to see her perform for others in a pool or pageant. I would've followed her anywhere.

I'd gained some skills. My body rolls were good, except for the side one. My favorite was the horizontal kick spin, and that was what I focused on the most.

In the water with Anemone cheering me on, coaching me, helping me, and asking me for help, I became beautiful. I became Starshell.

Starshell was lighthearted and silly. She could play in the water for hours and hours. She'd learned how to avoid ear and sinus infections (which involved an herbal concoction from Anemone and tips from Dr. Birdsong).

Starshell was a quicker wit than Amy Jay. She could rattle off puns all day, so long as she was in her tail. "We mermaid for each other," she'd say when Anemone made her face up like hers. "Shello, beautiful," she'd say, smiling with some food in her teeth.

Starshell didn't mind being laughed at when she was failing at performing a figure eight underwater. "You did a figure twelve," Anemone said with a giggle.

Starshell didn't mind the lake bros who threw clots of dirt at them because there were fewer of them than little girls who asked her if she was a real mermaid.

"My name is Starshell," she would say. "That's my friend Anemone. We're real mermaids."

I couldn't see Starshell no more. All I could see was old Amy Jay. In trouble again.

Heavy and forlorn, I glanced out over the lake, now forever a tomb, a memorial to poor Shimmerfish.

Starshell left me. I wished her well, and turned to face my new future.

* * *

"Guess we both have secrets now," Anemone said.

Two days. Two dead people. I was trapped in a terrible nightmare. An aqua-colored, glitter-smeared nightmare.

It took longer than you'd think for me to register what Anemone was telling me. I didn't comprehend the words coming out of her mouth. I was reeling from bumping into a floating corpse. Or, it bumping into me, I should say.

She talked and talked. Told me all about how the things she said about St. Germaine were all true.

Except she wasn't Phoebe/Shimmerfish.

Phoebe/Shimmerfish was dead.

The person whom I'd befriended had killed the girl that bobbed in the lukewarm water.

The person whom I'd befriended was not named Phoebe. She was not Dr. Birdsong's niece. The dead girl was Dr. Birdsong's niece.

The woman sobbing on the shore was named Madison.

"Like the mermaid in Splash," she said. "That's why Phoebe befriended me. Told me all about mermaids."

"*She* told *you*," I said out loud in the way one does when you're trying to suss something out. "You weren't into mermaids. She was." I pointed at the dead girl.

"Correct," she said. "She was Shimmerfish. She did all of this. We'd gotten on like a house afire until she wanted to come here."

"The stuff you said about her parents—true? They moved?"

Madison nodded. "It was fine. Clean slate. I'd been annoyed we had to come here in the first place. But Shimmerfish wanted to do her parents proud. Show off the bus she'd bought and built. Try to win back their love after they shipped her off to hell."

"She was the one with the bus."

Things began to make sense. None of this was hers. She didn't value it.

My mind wandered as it did in times of enormous stress. I could loosen my grip on reality when I needed to, and I needed to. Instead of thinking about the toxicity of this situation, I thought about the time I came home to find a baby grand piano on our front porch. Some relative had died and sent it to my dead momma, which sent her into a tizzy over why they didn't send the cash instead of the piano. According to the letter that accompanied it, the piano was a treasured heirloom, but everyone who cared for it had died.

I'd never seen an item so fine. The ebony wood shone in the afternoon sun, smooth and still cool to the touch. I loved to press the keys until the adults yelled to stop. I asked for lessons. Begged to bring it inside after a night of sleet and rain.

All fell on deaf ears.

I watched that beautiful instrument rot and decay while people came and went, storing things on it and in it. Dead plants. Gas cans. Trash of every variety.

A possum gave birth in it once, and the adults used the babies for target practice.

It collapsed into itself after a rainy summer. I helped smash it and throw it all on the wood pile.

You can't give things of value to people who ain't earned them. They don't care about them. That's what was happening with the turquoise bus. Madison was a shit bird shitting all over it because she didn't care nor understand the work that goes into nice things.

But Shimmerfish did.

The hair on the back of my neck stood up as I projected how the bus would fall into ruin. A small patch of rust would morph into a cancer. Broken windows wouldn't be replaced.

It dolphinately needed a new steering wheel.

Anemone didn't have what it took to preserve anything. To care for anything.

Anemone was a murderer.

A mer-durer.

"Why did you stay?" I asked.

"What do you mean?"

"After you did whatever you did to murder Shimmerfish you had no reason to stay. You could've left. Her parents didn't care about her. Her aunt hadn't seen her in years. It makes no fucking sense."

"She'd already called Dr. Birdsong and said she was coming," Anemone said, her eyes narrowing like a cartoon villain. "It's one of the things we fought about. And the fact that she was the mermaid, and I was the fucking pirate."

"You could've ghosted Dr. Birdsong," I said. "Why did you stay here?"

I was beginning to feel like I'd taken crazy pills. I needed rest. I needed answers.

"If someone claiming to be Phoebe didn't show up here within a few days, Dr. Birdsong would've called her parents. A search would've commenced. They would've found me and then," she drew her finger across her throat. "I've been locked up. That's not happening again. Ever."

Hearing her say her plan made it sound brilliant. Don't run. Don't hide. Become something else.

"I still don't understand why you stayed so long," I said, feeling the numbness take over my body like a storm cloud coming in over a vast expanse of sea.

She took a step toward me.

"Because of you," she said.

I didn't believe this for a good goddamn minute. But that didn't matter. I couldn't let on, lest I wanted to end up like Shimmerfish.

"And the benzos."

"The what?"

"I've been stealing pills from Dr. Birdsong. To sell. To fund my lifestyle."

Words escaped me.

"I loved Shimmerfish. I idolized her," Anemone continued, pleading with me to...what? Believe her? Forgive her?

"I don't care," I said. "Nothing matters now."

"Are you going to tell?"

"How did you kill her?"

"It was an accident, I swear."

"How does your friend end up rotting in a lake by accident? Then you took over her identity. I don't mean to upset you, *Madison*. But this seems calculated."

"What are you going to do?" Her tone had shifted.

"How did you kill her?" I pressed.

It was as if the blood froze in her veins. I believed her when she locked eyes with me and said, "Same way I'll kill you if you don't help me work this out. Push you in. Pull you under."

I had to play this carefully. I had one agenda, and that was to get myself out of town and away from whatever this was.

"You know what, Madison? I've had secrets, too. I know what it's like to be unable to trust anyone. I know what it's like to be abused and how the pain ignites a fury inside you."

The person standing before me seemed so much smaller to me now. I felt like I was dealing with a child.

"I knew you'd get it," she said.

"Oh, I do."

She took my hand, and we stood there, gazing at Shimmerfish's swollen, blue back. I wondered if it would pop if I poked it.

"Let's get out of here," she said.

"Like, forever?" I asked.

"Yes. You and me. Forever."

She leaned in close and kissed me on the lips. She tasted like fear. Metallic. Dirty.

"Forever," I said. "We're tied together forever now."

"I thought you'd see it my way. We're the same," she said.

"One quick thing."

"Yes?"

"I need my money back. Then we're going to go to the clinic."

"No," she said. "We need to get out of town."

"And leave my car there? We gotta take a page out of your play-book. We should go in like every day, everything's normal, nothing to see here. We'll lift any sellable items we can from Dr. Birdsong's stash. Then we'll dip. No one is looking for us yet. Let's play this out like nothing's wrong."

I didn't know whether this ruse would work or not, but it was the best I could come up with. It's challenging to strategize while looking at a decomposing corpse, and I don't recommend it to anyone.

Madison was unsure, so I pressed even further.

"If we both disappear this morning, Dr. Birdsong is going to send someone to my apartment and they're going to find Rutter there before lunchtime. That's not enough time for us to get away."

I saw her shoulders relax. I wasn't sure that was a good thing.

"Let's go, then," she said.

"First, we need to push her," I pointed at the dearly departed Phoebe/Shimmerfish. "Back out to sea. So to speak."

Chapter Nineteen

"Oh, and one more thing. Mermaiding is hot, sweaty, uncomfortable, painful, and dangerous. It's the best thing ever."
—Shimmerfish

Add to my list of disappointments with the so-called Anemone: she was too squeamish to push her dead friend back into the lake.

I did it myself, which now made me an accessory after the fact, a twist in the law I wouldn't learn until many years later.

But that's another story for another day.

Even in my childish ignorance, I knew what I was doing wasn't right. I'd hoped I'd find a way to come clean with Dr. Birdsong, with everyone.

Part of me thought it might be fitting to take one last spin in my tail whilst dragging the Shimmerfish back into her watery grave, but the clock was ticking.

While Anemone paced on the beach, I sat down in the shallows next to this rotting body, which smelled exactly like you think it would, and shoved my feet into my monofin.

"Coward," I muttered toward Anemone as I wiggled into the lake.

Shimmerfish's feet were floating in about a foot of water. I looked long and hard at those feet to try to gin up whatever courage it takes for a person to touch a dead body with their bare hands.

"I'm sorry about this, Shimmerfish," I said. "Would've been nice to know you. I adore your book. You were talented."

I'd gotten strong over the past weeks. I pulled Shimmerfish by her left ankle, praying the whole time the bottom part of her leg would stay attached. When we got to the tree branches where we'd first made our acquaintance, I dove underwater and dragged her beneath the surface. It took a couple of tries, many breaths, and a superhuman ability to compartmentalize trauma in order for me to get her fluke wedged between a few branches. Bodies bloat. Try pulling a balloon underwater and tying it to a branch. That's what I was dealing with.

"I'm so sorry," I said to the surface of the water when my dark deed was done.

And I was.

I was so, so sorry.

* * *

The bouncy motion of the bus on the way back to town was a direct counterpoint to my dark mood. My plan was not failsafe. Anemone was unpredictable.

We pulled into the clinic parking lot and were set upon by the largest group of protesters I'd ever seen. They were yelling things like *don't you want your child to grow up to ride a school bus* and *I will adopt your baby* and other less flattering things about our looks, weight, and intelligence.

"*Murderers!*" they screeched.

And they were right.

About one of us anyway.

"Well?" I said.

"Well, *what*?" she said.

"I want my money."

"Oh, that? I can keep it safe. Trust me."

"Trust is something we may need to build," I said.

"Alright then." She handed me half of the wad. "You take half. Then, I want you to get in your sad Volkswagen beetle and drive away from here. I'll tell Dr. Birdsong you're not feeling well. Should buy you a couple of days so long as Rutter doesn't start to smell."

I gritted my teeth and pocketed the dough. I was big mad, but I knew better than to argue now.

We'd sort this out, one way or another.

The protesters had clustered around the front of the bus.

When the door opened, the crowd parted, and Anemone maneuvered me toward the area where my car was parked, her grip tight on my upper arm.

As she dragged me along, I noticed the W was missing from the sign again.

Vexing. But I didn't have time to ruminate on the reasons why grown adults behaved like rabid toddlers.

"This girl wants an abortion!" Anemone shouted. "Imma put her in her car and send her to church!"

Red meat to the slavering mob.

"What are you—"

The crowd moved with a hive mind across the parking lot to where Anemone had me in a death grip. She held me still while the crowd spat at me, hit me with signs, called me names. I was mute from exhaustion. My goal was to break free from her mer-grip and scurry into the clinic, where I could spill my guts to Dr. Birdsong.

"What in all of botheration is going on out here?"

Dr. Birdsong's voice rose above the cacophony. Anemone continued to drag me toward my dead momma's vee-dub-ya, but we'd been made, and there was no way she could explain her actions to the good doctor.

I focused on Dr. Birdsong's voice as Anemone froze in the middle of the scrum. I feared they'd tear us limb from limb. Their eyes were afire with the fury of their hateful god. Every molecule of their malevolent energy was directed at me.

"Your mama's a murderer!" I heard Dr. Birdsong shriek. "Clovis, go home! Your wife thinks you're at work right now."

Then, in a lower voice, her hand on my lower back, guiding me, "Come with me."

I wasn't aware if Anemone was following us through the chaos, and I didn't care. The relief I felt, standing in the lobby with the sound of the protesters outside, was real.

I didn't even mind when Dr. Birdsong let Anemone in.

She'd fetched the remaining protection spells we'd hidden and lobbed them at the roiling crowd before slamming the door and locking it behind her.

"They're insane," she said, out of breath.

We had some things to sort out.

The three of us stood in silence for longer than was comfortable, the sounds of the raging crowd our soundtrack. The clinic interior was in the same condition we'd left it: demolished.

I stood on broken glass. Tried not to gape at the destruction we still needed to clean up. Those people outside were angry and they meant business.

And Madison/Anemone had sicced them on me.

Finally, Dr. Birdsong spoke.

"So, ladies. What's new?"

Standing there in the spotlight of Dr. Birdsong's furious gaze made me feel three feet tall.

Anemone's mouth seemed to be broken. We eyeballed each other, daring the other one to say anything.

"Well?"

Dr. Birdsong's arms were crossed. She tapped her foot. She looked at her watch.

"Seeing as you seem to be experiencing a case of sudden onset mutism, I'm going to tell you what I saw," she said. "Anemone, it looked like you were doing a bang-up job of working the crowd into a froth by claiming that your colleague was coming in for an abortion. I'm gobsmacked that I need to point out the obvious stupidity of your behavior, considering we don't even do abortions here. You could've gotten hurt, injured, maimed, or worse. Those people are thirsty for blood, and they have more guns between them than many small nations have in their entire armies. What you did, Anemone, was the equivalent of covering Amy Jay in blood and dropping her into a bear pit."

"But she—" Anemone began.

Dr. Birdsong put a finger up. "I will not hear it," she said. "I don't care what Amy Jay did. You put her in the direct line of danger for what? A prank? Tomfoolery? You girls have a spat? You put me in a bad position. And you need to tell me right now why I shouldn't fire you."

Some things I'd never experienced were happening. First of all, ain't no one ever taken up for me when something went wrong. My hackles were up, and I was ready to do anything to save myself, even if it meant telling Dr. Birdsong everything. And I did mean everything. I didn't care if she fired me, so long as she didn't think I'd ever disrespect her. I'd made some mistakes, but they were honest ones. I couldn't tolerate the thought of Dr. Birdsong thinking less of me.

But before I could formulate a thought, Anemone opened her yap and let out a tall tale to cover her own ass. I couldn't even figure out why. She wasn't related to Dr. Birdsong, could leave whenever she wanted. But somehow, she thought she needed to throw me under the bus, reference intended.

"Amy Jay's sixteen years old," Anemone said. "Did you know that? Her name's not even Amy Jay. It's Madison. And she murdered her boyfriend last night. I saw the whole thing after she did a hex on my bus. She's dangerous and insane. I'm trying to protect you, Aunt Robin. Like you've done for me. My parents are gone. You're all I've got."

That's the sentimental stuff Dr. Birdsong fell for every time.

Dr. Birdsong embraced Anemone. Anemone held her middle finger up to me behind Dr. Birdsong's back.

The room went blurry. My teeth tingled and my eyes burned. I felt a separation happen between my mind and my body. I was experiencing an intense calm, the kind you slip into when you're about to do something brave or something terrible—or when you're dying. My entire life was suspended before me by a powerful force I now recognize as survival. A crossroads yawned before me. And it was my choice whether I had a future or if I continued to let shit weasels like Anemone determine how I turned out.

The light in the room sharpened. I could smell the disinfectant we used to clean the bathroom. I could hear the medical table paper rustling under the air conditioning.

"Is this true, Amy Jay?" Dr. Birdsong looked into my eyes. "Or should I say, *Madison?*"

The look on her face was pure pain.

Anemone smirked.

"I'm sixteen," I began. "And I'm so sorry. You never asked, so I never told. And about the rest of it, that bitch is full of it, and here's what happened."

I was in two places. I was there, in the clinic, getting ready to speak more than I ever had. But I was also with my dead momma.

The confused, overawed look on Anemone's face reminded me of the time my dead momma got gangrene in her small toe from using dirty tools to give herself a pedicure on the back porch. It was coming off; she was losing her toe. But as they came to get her and put her in the wheelchair, she asked, "How long will it take, after?"

The doctor replied, "You'll heal for a few weeks. Change the dressings, make sure you keep it clean."

"No," she said. "How long till it grows back?"

Anemone had the same look. Total disbelief at what she was hearing.

She didn't think I had it in me.

But I did. I'd already died once in this life. And seen two dead bodies in twenty-four hours, one of them a human dressed like some tuna.

Nothing scared me now.

I opened my mouth, and I started to talk, but there was no sound, only the opening and closing of my jaw, like a fish gulping for oxygen after being yanked from its watery home.

Dr. Birdsong looked at me like I was the devil. I understood. We're inclined to believe our relatives in such matters, and she was hearing a lot of new stuff about me she'd never thought to ask. Never mind it was all made up, except the age part.

I spoke, and it was like dropping a glass container full of marbles on the floor. Information bounced all over, every which way. No one was spared.

I told Dr. Birdsong everything, including my age and all the stuff about my dead momma and Rutter, Madison, Anemone, Phoebe and Shimmerfish—everything I knew about how Anemone had taken on Phoebe/Shimmerfish's life as her own, using the information Dr. Birdsong hadn't seen her niece in years to get in here to steal drugs from her cabinet, which she should lock, by the way.

Dr. Birdsong appeared to age twenty years. Then, she said, "Amy Jay, I'm a mandated reporter, do you know what that means?"

"Unfortunately, ma'am, I do."

She took her glasses off and rubbed her eyes the way adults do when they're forced to deal with something they didn't see coming. "I'm sorry to say I will be forced to report this. I take no pleasure in it. But you've lied. And you're a child. You need adult supervision. A clean place to live. My god, I can't believe I let you live alone in a tenement."

I looked over at Anemone, who couldn't believe her good luck.

"I don't need parents," I said. "Rutter was the reason I came here in the first place. My momma died and, well, you know what happened to me. Please, don't do this. Anemone is a full-on murderer."

"Amy Jay, it's not up to me. I could lose my license. I can't believe I didn't know. You don't look sixteen."

My entire body jolted in fear. "All I wanted to do was work here. With you. You're so kind. And then, and then..."

I'd begun to say the name *Anemone*, but I couldn't formulate the syllables, now I knew it was all a lie.

"...I met her. And she showed me all about mermaiding and mer-witching, and I've never been a part of something more magical in all my life. But, Dr. Birdsong. She's not Phoebe. She killed your niece, and her dead body is out there right now in a silicone mermaid tail, decomposing in a stand of submerged tree branches at Lake Longago."

"She's lying," Anemone said. "She's the murderer. She killed Phoebe. She also killed her boyfriend. Last night."

"Stop saying he was my boyfriend," I said. I couldn't even with her description of Rutter and she got me so worked up, I stomped on her foot and pushed her backwards like the bullies at school used to do to me.

I reared back to drop a punch in the middle of her forehead when Dr. Birdsong grabbed me.

"Amy Jay, no," Dr. Birdsong pulled me, and we both stumbled backwards.

Anemone stayed where she'd fallen. She curled into a ball, as if she were trying to disappear.

Silence.

We exchanged glances.

"Where'd the protesters go?" I asked.

Madison laughed. A dark sound. "Home to wash."

I knew better.

My blood curdled. My heart felt like it'd come down with a fever.

Silence was never good.

If they left, they were coming back.

Then, a clinking sound on the floor, like a bottle rolling across tile.

Strange, I thought, as I turned to see a metal object, wrapped with tape. Under the tape, nails, screws, washers, pennies.

A reverse protection spell. The shrapnel is on the outside.

I smiled at the symmetry of my situation.

Then, a flash of recognition appeared on Dr. Birdsong's face as she screamed for us to run.

We raced to the door, but it was too late.

The boom was a jackboot on my back. A sound that was more of a feeling rattled my teeth and vibrated in my bones. So loud I didn't even hear it. I remember the ringing. Ringing like my head was inside a church bell. Intense ringing came from inside my skull, not my ears. My ears were broken.

I was hit from the side. Glass, stone, heat, sharp bits of a pipe bomb. The force of it lifted me off my feet and ferried me through the wall as it collapsed.

I came to face-first on the small, grassy incline behind the clinic.

I'd been dead before.

I didn't die this time.

Couldn't say the same for Dr. Birdsong. Or Anemone.

Soon, I could hear the wee-woo wagons coming in the distance. A countdown. I had to act fast.

Whoever had tossed the pipe bomb had gotten the fuck out of Dodge, and so had all the stragglers.

So much for pro-life, I thought as I pulled myself up. Leaving three women out here for dead.

I scrambled over to Dr. Birdsong, whose body was mangled like the gods had chewed her up and spit her back to earth. Her arms and legs bent at odd angles, a week-old dead spider. I told her I was sorry, and I thanked her. I didn't dare plumb the depths of the feelings I'd experience for Dr. Birdsong. My angel. I never would've gotten up if I had.

I had to hurry.

When I got to Anemone, I tried not to look.

I took her shoes. Slipped them onto my feet. Put my shoes on hers.

Removed her cross-body bag. Checked for her ID and the money she owed me. All there.

And the keys to the bus.

I took off my backpack. Put it on her.

Dipped my hand in the blood that pooled around her head (which had popped open like a cherry tomato). Rubbed it all over the backpack.

The sirens closed in.

"*So mote it be*, Madison," I said. "You blowhole."

Every joint in my body cried out in pain as I hobbled toward the turquoise bus.

The Women's Whole Health sign had been blown into the parking lot. It was blocking the bus, its second W still missing.

I accessed my white trash strength to grab that menacing sign and drag it out of the way. Dipped my fingers into the blood that was streaming down my neck. Scratched a capital dub-ya in dark, red blood. Then I went over it again for good measure.

"Better," I said to no one.

The bus awaited me like an old friend. I climbed aboard. Patted the loose steering wheel.

"Let's go, old girl. We got this."

I started the bus. Maneuvered it away from the sound of the sirens. Toward the ocean I'd never seen.

I bounced along the road on my way to...Tampa, maybe? I drove and formulated the fiction I'd tell about how a mermaid once saved me.

Thought about adding to the book.

WHEN YOU ARRIVE IN TAMPA
    Get driver's license.
    Find mer-pod first thing.
    Get job.
    Save for silicone tail that changes color in the sun.
    Mer. All day. All night.

I'd been dead once before, and dead-adjacent twice after.
    This time, I was going to live my life. And hers.
    Shimmerfish, I become you. Shimmerfish, I honor you.
    So mote it be.

END

Acknowledgments

George Dondero, you're an exceptional beta reader, cover designer, marketing consultant, animator, film director, and so much more. I appreciate your eye for detail and your constant, unwavering support. Kirsten Smith, thank you for always taking the time to read and critique my work. Leah Eichler, you've been a huge support from the beginning. Linda Shaw, thank you for always being positive about my writing—and everything else! And, finally, my endless gratitude to everyone who reads, recommends, and reviews my stories, and to every book lover who supports indie authors.

Visit my site at bethanybrowning.com. And if you read and enjoyed *Shimmerfish*, please leave a review!

About the Author

Bethany Browning lives and works in a redwood forest. Her debut horror novella, *Sasquatch, Baby!*, and the first in her cozy mystery series, *Dead Spread*, are both available in eBook and paperback. Plus, *War of the Wills*, a film she co-wrote with George Dondero, is watchable on Amazon Prime. Her award-nominated short fiction can be found in *Halloween Horrors, Stories We Tell After Midnight, The HallowZine, Mudroom, JAKE, Filth, Reckon Review, Esoterica, Flash Fiction Magazine* and dozens more. For more information and to read her short stories and other published work, visit bethanybrowning.com and follow her on Threads @bethanybrowningbooks.

Bonus Content

FOREST BATHING
by Bethany Browning

Elvira didn't mind when the centipede nibbled a hole through her eardrum. She appreciated the feathery feel of its itty-bitty feet as it tiptoed into her sinuses, where it laid twenty-six eggs and curled its body around them until they hatched. Eventually, the offspring unfurled through her nasal cavity like fortunes from a cookie.

She knew no one lived forever. But no one, not even her Oma who obsessed over TV true crime shows, ever mentioned how the body rots if it's left lifeless in a crushed heap under the fallen branch of a redwood tree. The way it stiffens (uncomfortable). The off-gassing (noisome). The bloat (embarrassing).

No one ever mentioned the dangers inherent in forest bathing, or shinrin-yoku, as her co-worker Beth called it, with more of an accent than Elvira thought H.R. would approve of.

Elvira was a city girl. She was only on this solitary outing because her job selling vacation timeshares was frustrating, exhausting, and possibly criminal. She despised her flatulent boss and her cheerful colleagues. Her clients were the kind of folksy folks who believed that a one-bedroom apartment in Cabo, available twice a year, was the height of vacation sophistication.

She'd stopped looking at herself in the mirror.

"Shinrin-yoku," Beth had said. "Go for a slow walk in the redwoods. Bask in the negative ions. Increases serotonin."

Elvira had nothing to lose, so she piloted her Prius through rush hour traffic to the unpaved parking lot at the Old Grove and took a forest bath, an activity commonly known as *walking*.

The first thing she noticed was the aroma: bracing, piney. The next thing she noticed was the silence, a sharp contrast to the roar of the city where her senses were assaulted by the droning of buses, the beeping of construction vehicles, and the continual shrieking of car alarms.

Even a broken clock's right twice a day, she thought, about Beth. Elvira felt restored enough to walk the entire two-mile loop, and when she was done with that, she ventured off the trail, into the thick of the forest where the floor was spongy with detritus, the trees were close-together, and no one would ever find her.

The last thing she noticed was the smile on her face. The last thing she heard was the crack of the branch.

Elvira was gone in the time it takes to say, "Sign here."

It wasn't like the movies, where the disembodied former person floats above their corpse, watching things unfold. The 'she' that she once was was *still in there*, experiencing the deterioration of her meat body as what made her *her* transformed into energy.

Elvira felt better than she had in ages.

She was aware that critters were devouring her flesh. From scavengers with piercing beaks to microbes, maggots, and mites, she placidly endured their stabbing, tugging, tickling, and snuffling. It was fascinating to be *thisclose* to a pack of coyotes who licked her shin bones clean before dragging them off to their den for their pups to gnaw on.

She was experiencing feelings without having feelings, which was the oddest feeling of all.

With nothing but time to think, Elvira realized—too late—as she rested in this void, this stillness outside of time: her life had been a waste.

She'd focused on all the wrong things. In childhood, it was one-upping her friends by cheating at games or mocking them behind their backs. In middle school, she'd stop at nothing to be the center of attention. In high school, her main goal was hooking up with boys. College? Too hard. She was a bad employee (unmotivated, easily bored, gossipy) and had been fired from five jobs.

Elvira hadn't seen or spoken to Oma in six months. Barely thought of her now that she was in assisted living.

She believed her behavior might be the result of being depressed, that her anxieties about work and money and dating and debt were keeping her stuck in a pattern of selfishness. But she never did anything about any of it. Trudged along day after day, never improving, never changing. Drinking more. Sleeping less.

She should've been a better granddaughter and a better friend. Sent *thank you* notes. Refrained from seducing her besties' boyfriends and husbands. Told her cousin that she dropped his baby onto the floor when she was babysitting (he seemed fine?). She reconsidered her disastrous decision to call the cops on her neighbor's yipping Maltese (R.I.P. Dumpling). If she had a do-over, she'd stop herself from telling that girl to kill herself on Instagram.

Failures and character flaws appeared before her like a slide show. She hadn't been a serious person. The her that once was Elvira was a narcissist and a troll, and she regretted it.

As she rested there, rotting and releasing, she marveled at her refreshed sense of purpose. Her cells unraveled, her senses expanded. Every being that arrived to devour her was a chattering friend, inviting her into the earth, bringing bits of her into the understory, into their nests, nourishing their offspring with her nails, her corneas, her brain, her blood, her mucous. She was infused with their gratitude, and she witnessed life thrumming through each of them. Her body had been transformed into life for millions of other living things. Next spring, this spot would flourish with lush green growth from the nitrogen her biomatter left behind.

Elvira finally mattered.

Over time, only a scattering of brittle bones remained. Elvira was pulled to merge what remained of the her that was *her* into the yawning mouth of everything there was. Confident that there was nothing more to fear, and done with her meaningless leftovers, Elvira exhaled into the what-comes-next, promising to do better.

END

You've never seen a custody battle like this. After her posh Napa Valley friends cut her off for committing an unspeakable betrayal, Tabitha Eggs retreats to the redwood forests of Del Norte County, California, to drink herself to death. But when she stumbles over two decomposing corpses near her new home, she believes that walking into a wildfire is preferable to whatever waits in the woods. Her plans are foiled when she's kept alive by a curious Sasquatch, and they create a bizarre and everlasting union.

When tarot card reader Carrie Dettwiler stumbles across the mayor's dead body on a random Tuesday, town gossip reaches a fever pitch—and everyone's convinced she and her rescue raven Waggery have performed a deadly dark ritual. Carrie deals with the cards she's been dealt, turning over every clue, only to be blown off course by her gale-force feelings for tattoo artist Stormy Portwood, who breezes into town at the same time people start dying. Determined to divine the criminal who's terrorizing the citizens of Prosperity, Carrie must rely on her dangerous knowledge of the town's secret history to reveal the killer.

Edited by Blair Daniels. HALLOWEEN HORRORS is a wildly terrifying anthology of Halloween stories. Ghoulish trick-or-treaters, gruesome jack o'lanterns, and faceless specters haunt the pages of this book, ready to leap to life in the deepest corners of your mind. Sit down in front of the fire, as the chilly autumn wind howls outside, and read... if you dare.

Edited by Rachel Brune. From deserted islands to an isolated cabin in the Carolina woods, from an Arizona film set to a small Mexican town, from a bloody riverbank in Vietnam to the coal-choked streets of Cheapside, the Stories We Tell After Midnight series has invited the reader into a world of shadows almost forgotten by the cold glare of the modern world. This, the third and final volume of the series, offers up more tales of revenge, of hunger, and of the false light of redemption—but only to those who once more dare turn the page.